WHITEWATER DEATH!

The raft thumped over a submerged rock, nearly tossing Kit and Mark overboard. Overhead the sky narrowed to a jagged, blue slit as the walls compressed against the river, angering it as the canyon darkened.

"Hold on!" Kit tightened his grip on one of the ropes that lashed the logs together. Already the logs were loosening and beginning to grind against one another. Suddenly the raft plunged a dozen feet. It momentarily dove beneath the cold water, then burst through the surface, nearly flipping over. For an instant it hung in the suction of the falls, spinning wildly, then shot as if from a cannon into a chute of tumbling water. Kit and Mark gasped for air as the roaring of the water pounded their ears and echoed up the canyon walls like the impish laughter of all the ghosts of all those ancients who had run this water before—and had died beneath its foaming face.

"This is it, Kit!" Mark shouted. "This river is gonna kill us!"

The *Kit Carson* series:
THE COLONEL'S DAUGHTER

KIT CARSON

#2:
GHOSTS OF
LODORE
Doug Hawkins

LEISURE BOOKS   NEW YORK CITY

For Virgil Collins

A LEISURE BOOK®

November 1997

Published by

Dorchester Publishing Co., Inc.
276 Fifth Avenue
New York, NY 10001

If you purchased this book without a cover you should be aware that this book is stolen property. It was reported as "unsold and destroyed" to the publisher and neither the author nor the publisher has received any payment for this "stripped book."

Copyright © 1997 by Dorchester Publishing Co., Inc.

All rights reserved. No part of this book may be reproduced or transmitted in any form or by any electronic or mechanical means, including photocopying, recording or by any information storage and retrieval system, without the written permission of the Publisher, except where permitted by law.

ISBN 0-8439-4325-4

The name "Leisure Books" and the stylized "L" with design are trademarks of Dorchester Publishing Co., Inc.

Printed in the United States of America.

ACKNOWLEDGMENT

My sincerest thanks to the late Dr. Thomas Edward, who so graciously allowed me to roam freely through his rare and valuable collection of monographs by that nineteenth century Native American scholar, Professor W. G. F. Smith.

ACKNOWLEDGMENTS

KIT CARSON

#2:
GHOSTS OF
LODORE

Chapter One

The stout wind buffeted the back of his buckskin shirt almost as if with malevolent intent, trying to nudge him forward. He took another tentative step toward the sharp precipice and leaned over ever so cautiously. With one hand he anchored the flapping brim of his black beaver hat. The dizzying drop-off that widened before his eyes sent an electric current of thrill shooting through him! It was always like this for Kit Carson when coming face-to-face with eternity, as he did now.

But still he wasn't satisfied.

He was bound to tempt fate, and the steadfastness of his own legs, to the limit. Bracing himself upon his long J. J. Henry rifle, Kit tilted forward just one . . . more . . . small . . . degree farther . . .

For a moment he teetered upon the brink of eternity, floating above the bottomless gorge that opened below him. All at once Kit let loose a long, heartfelt whistle and backed away from the sheer drop-off. "That thar's got to be the deepest gouge the Good Lord ever did cut into his green earth!" he proclaimed as he made his way back to his horse, noting wryly that Joe Meek was inching up to the brink on all fours. And a few feet in the other direction, Newell, who was generally known among the trappers as the "doctor," had taken a healthy hold onto the tenacious branch of a nearby scrub oak before risking a peak over the edge at the glistening thread of water two thousand feet below.

The Crow Indians had a name for it; the Seedskee-dee Agie—the Sage Hen River. But because of its color, most of the white trappers just generally called it the Green.

Jim Bridger had remained upon his horse, a safe distance back, along with Waldo Gray Feather Smith and Mark Head. Bridger only frowned at Kit's declaration, looking sober as always. Some thought that the Archangel Gabriel was a somber creature too; hence Bridger's nickname, "Gabe."

"Why, that's jest a baby canyon, Kit. I reckon you ain't never seen the Great Canyon of the Colorado, now have you?"

"Heard of it, Gabe, though I admit I've never been there. Someday I'll go have me a visit. I hear tell it shines." Kit shoved a foot into the stirrup and swung up onto his horse.

"It shines, all right. Puts this here slit in the ground to shame, it do, and that's the truth."

"Maybe so, but the way I see it, be it only a mile wide or be it twenty miles wide, unless we sprout wings, and these packhorses too, it's a mighty big ditch to be jumping."

For an instant a grin worked its way onto Bridger's face; then the frown returned. "North of here a little way we climb down off of these cliffs and come to wide river bottom. We'll make the crossing there, at a place called the Gates."

Meek and Newell came back from the edge of the canyon as a few of the other men of the party still strolled along its ragged rim, trying to get a look at the river, which was shrunk by distance to a mere line scratched along the bottom of the canyon.

"No matter how many times I've seen it," Joe Meek was saying, "I never get over how spectacular the view is from up here."

Waldo Gray Feather Smith, the half-breed Ute whose white father had made a small fortune in shipping on the Erie Canal and then sent his son to Harvard for a "proper" education, had remained firmly planted upon his saddle. "This is about as close as I care to get, gentlemen."

Newell laughed. "You ain't scared of heights, Gray Feather, are you?"

"Afraid of heights? Not at all. I just have a healthy respect for the law of gravity."

Joe Meek climbed back aboard his cayuse. "Don't have to worry none 'bout that here. Last I hear'd, there warn't no law west of the Missouri River."

The men laughed, while Gray Feather only grinned and nodded his head. "If that's so, why did I see you creeping up on that brink as if it were a sleeping wildcat?"

"Because I hold a healthy respect for wildcats," Meek answered.

Kit rocked back in his saddle, laughing. "Whal, law or no, it's time we start making our way down to that river if we're ever going to get there before nightfall." He slanted an eye towards Jim Bridger. "How are you fixing to do it anyway, Gabe? Even from way up here, it's plain that wild river is swol-

11

len with spring snowmelt and bucking like a green mustang."

The Englishman, Perry Swingle, urged his horse forward a few steps and pulled up alongside Kit and Bridger. "It's a roiling mess down there, gov'ner. Reckon we might find still water farther north?"

Bridger nodded. "I've crossed this here crik a time or two during the spring runs. It's got high water, all right, but the channel's deep before it plunges into this canyon—about a dozen miles up-river from here. When we get there we'll fell some trees and fix us up a raft of cottonwoods. In the mornin' we'll run a rope to the other side and pull the company across in shifts."

Swingle looked doubtful, but he kept his skepticism to himself. "Whatever you say. You're Booshway of this here company."

The other men had saddled up by then. Bridger turned the party of trappers away from the rocky, wind-scoured escarpment, and a few hours later they rode out of the broken landscape onto the flat, barren country bordering that part of the Green River. The camp keepers began setting up camp while Bridger and Meek went off to survey a stand of timber and select the trees that would be suitable to make into a raft to ferry the company of men and the packhorses, heavy with two dozen bundles of beaver plews and equipment, across the high, swift water of the Green River.

Kit Carson, Gray Feather, and Mark Head climbed over the shelves of sandstone to the river's edge and stood there a few minutes, watching the racing torrent. As they looked on, a tree, ripped up from somewhere upstream, bobbed past on the swift current of water fed by the high-country run-off, its branches clutching at rocks as if pleading for deliverance.

Gray Feather said, "Not a good season to be crossing this river. The river ghosts are drunk with the snowmelt."

"River ghosts?" Mark laughed and tossed a stone out into the fast water, the sound of it disappearing below, lost in the steady, low roar. "Is that an old Ute yarn?"

Gray Feather looked at him curiously, a small grin moving across his face. "It's from the literature of Europe, actually. Germanic in origin, I believe."

The smile faded from Mark's lips, and now it was Kit's turn to give a short laugh. "Reckon I ought to have warned you about Gray Feather, Mark. He ain't like no other Injun you ever met, and that's the truth. He's went to a college to learn about the kinda books folks read in England. He's got a head full of words big enough t' choke a buffler, and he's particularly bothersome when it comes to quoting Shakespeare and the Bible."

"That's all fine and good, I reckon. But can he shoot?"

"Some. I've seen him part one of Yellow Wolf's Dog Soldiers' topknot once, and he keeps a cool head."

"I reckon he'll do then."

Gray Feather cleared his throat. "I'm beginning to feel like nothing more than a pronoun."

Both trappers gave Gray Feather a blank look. He grinned, glanced back at the roiling waters and said:

And thumping and plumping and bumping
   and jumping,

*And dashing and flashing and splashing and
   clashing;
And so never ending, but always descending,
Sounds and motions for ever and ever are
   blending,
All at once and all o'er, with a mighty uproar,
And this way the Water comes down at Lodore.*

"What's that all about?" Kit asked.

"It's from a child's poem by England's poet laureate Robert Southey. The poem is titled *The Cataract of Lodore*. This wild river, and the rapids in that canyon, just sort of reminded me of the poem."

"The Cataract of Lodore," Kit repeated to himself as if trying the words out for his own use. "I sorta like the sound of that." He glanced at the towering cliffs at the entrance of the canyon that compressed the river. "Gabe just calls them the Gates. I reckon I'll call them the Gates of Lodore."

The sound of chopping turned their heads. Kit said, "They're gonna need a hand cuttin' down them trees," and leaving the riverbank, they took up axes and went to work felling the timber that was to make up the raft.

The rest of that day a fifteen-by-twenty-foot raft took shape in a cove of relatively still water. The raft was anchored to the shore by two ropes while each log was floated in place and lashed tight to the preceding one. By nightfall the job was finished. Exhausted, the men ate in the light of a fire and immediately crawled off to their blankets. It seemed to Kit as if he had only just fallen asleep when he was suddenly awaken by Bridger's voice.

"Levé, leché, lego," the Booshway shouted, moving among the sleeping forms as a pink glow was

14

spreading up the eastern sky. *"Levé, leché, lego.* Up and at 'em, boys. Got a long day ahead of us."

By the time the sun was full in the sky, they had eaten and were preparing for the crossing. Joe Meek took one end of a rope, leaped onto his stout Indian pony, and rode several hundred feet up the river and plunged in. The horse swam hard against the current as the river carried them relentlessly toward the towering pillars of rock on either side where the channel narrowed and the water, as if resenting the contraction of its channel, turned angry. Bridger called that fissure in the mountain the Gates, although Kit had never heard the place called by any other name but "Hell's Canyon."

Joe made the crossing safely, and with the rope tied around a thick cottonwood tree up on the bank, Perry Swingle and Silas Klemper took their horses on board the raft and hauled themselves across the swift current. Then, with a crew of strong shoulders and arms on both sides of the river, Bridger ordered the six packhorses carrying the precious beaver packs onto the raft. He put Robert Newell with them, and Gray Feather, because of his innate feel for horses, acquired while growing up among the Utes.

As the raft slowly made the crossing, Kit watched for the uprooted trees that occasionally passed by. They halted once to let a battering ram of jagged roots flow by the raft, then started up again, and in short order the packhorses were safely scrambling onto dry ground. The raft came back across. Bridger was favoring his right arm after the hard pull, and Kit figured that the arrowhead that was still lodged in the mountain man's back from a scuffle with the Gros Ventre at Pierre's Hole three years earlier was acting up again.

15

Bridger glanced at Kit and Mark. "Looks like we're the last ones, boys." They took their horses onto the raft, holding the reins firmly when the animals became suddenly skittish at the moving deck beneath them. Giving the signal, Bridger released the rope on their end, relying now on the five men already across the river to pull them across. Caught in the current's mighty fist, the raft slowly swung out in a long arc at the end of the rope.

Mark Head's face paled as the raft picked up speed.

"Don't much care for this, do ya?" Bridger observed.

Mark swallowed hard. "I know it's kinda late to bring this up now, Gabe, but the truth of the matter is, I can't swim."

Kit stepped in to steady the trapper, who had gone suddenly rigid. He'd known Mark for two years, and had saved his life earlier that year in a battle with the Blackfeet over some stolen horses. Kit had taken a bullet in his shoulder for his efforts in that battle, and the wound was only now healed enough for him to regain full use of the arm. Without question, Mark was a brave man . . . almost to the point of sheer recklessness. He had once leaped after a wounded grizzly bear to finish the beast off. But now, as he was being jostled about on this raft, all that grit had faded away. His eyes had widened fearfully, his knuckles whitening on the reins.

"We're almost across," Kit said in a calm voice that he hoped would put his friend at ease.

Through some mystery of suction, a tree torn out by its roots had been drawn down below the surface. Perhaps in the deep a rock had intervened and broken the river's sinking hold on it. Whatever the reason, all at once it surged to the surface, a spider's web of naked roots bursting into view. The problem with being pulled across the river at the end of a rope, tugged downstream like a cork on a fishing line, was that there was no way to control your passage. Before, when the rope had been anchored on both sides of the river, stopping for a passing snag was no problem. Now it was nearly impossible. There was no avoiding this missile, and the next instant it caromed into the raft, jolting it out of its way.

Caught by the impact unexpectedly, Bridger reeled into the boiling water. The raft lifted on its far corner. The horses reared, and the next moment all three of them were in the water and kicking frantically toward the near shore. Kit grabbed Mark's arm tighter as the impact knocked both men to the deck. He turned a loose end of rope around his hands and then held on. The raft buckled as if nature had suddenly set them down upon the back of a wild stallion. The upthrust of roots slipped past, and just as Kit figured the worst had passed, the gnarled wood suddenly caught on the guide rope, and with its weight and velocity of the water propelling it, the rope strained, groaned, and snapped!

The raft shot ahead, held mercilessly in the river's mighty grip, wheeling wildly. Kit caught a glimpse of Jim Bridger's head bobbing in the water, and of the three horses nearing the shore; then the raft took a couple of turns and his eyes all at once were riveted upon the Gates . . . Kit's "Gates of Lodore" . . . the entrance into Hell's Canyon!

"We gotta jump, Mark," Kit shouted above the rising crescendo of crashing water.

"I can't!"

"I won't let you drown."

Mark shook his head. A sudden plunge sent a wall

17

of icy water crashing over them. "I'll never make it, Kit," he sputtered. "You go before it's too late."

Kit wouldn't leave him there on the raft alone, and anyway, the time for escape was swiftly passing. Even the most powerful swimmer couldn't escape the iron grip of this water now. "We'll have to ride it out!" Kit shouted over the roar of the river. In the short time left he managed to lash their rifles to one of the logs. Then the canyon's walls rose up on either side and the air grew colder as their shadows closed in around them.

Chapter Two

At first it was only a fast, bumpy ride as the high waters rushed them into the canyon. Then the river took a sharp turn, widened a few hundred feet, and slowed a little. Kit figured a strong swimmer might reach the little bits of rocky shore that ran back a few dozen feet before the canyon walls shot straight up. He could make it, but Mark would surely founder in the attempt and be swept into the narrows ahead.

Now past the first rapids, Kit stood to survey the river and search for some way to pilot the raft toward the rocky shore. Mark sat up, holding the loose piece of rope as if it were a lifeline. The deck had been swept clean of all their supplies except the rifles, still tied securely, and what each man carried. What Kit needed was some kind of rudder, a pole perhaps. Would a rifle be enough for the task? Kit didn't think so. Suddenly the water took on a eerie, pale green luminosity, as if somehow it was being lit by a big fire below.

Ahead, the roar of rushing water grew louder. Mark glanced up at Kit and managed a grimace. "I'd as soon face a passel of Blackfeet Injuns than go through that, Kit."

The current still had them trapped, and Kit still hadn't figured out a way to break free of it and propel the raft into shore. "This is sorta like being caught in the middle of a stampeding buffler herd, Mark," Kit said. "All we can do is ride it out."

Mark wiped the dripping hair from his eyes. "I've ridden out a buffler stampede once, Kit. It ain't something I care to do again."

The raft thumped over a submerged rock, nearly tossing Kit overboard. Overhead the sky narrowed to a jagged, blue slit as the walls compressed against the river, angering it as the canyon darkened. Sunlight would only reach this stretch of water for a few hours in the middle of the day; gloom would reign the rest of the time.

"Hold On!" Kit tightened his grip on one of the ropes that lashed the logs together. Already the logs were loosening and beginning to grind against one another. Suddenly the raft plunged a dozen feet. It momentarily dove beneath the cold water, then burst through the surface, nearly flipping over. For an instant it hung in the suction of the falls, spinning wildly, then shot as if from a cannon into a chute of tumbling water. Kit and Mark gasped for air as the roaring of the water pounded their ears and echoed up the canyon walls like the impish laughter of all the ghosts of all those ancients who had run this water before—and had died beneath its foaming face.

"This is it, Kit!" Mark shouted. "This river is gonna kill us!"

But Kit wasn't about to give in so easily. The water dumped them over another rocky cataract, dashing the raft against huge boulders that strained the ever-weakening ropes. The logs had begun to move beneath Kit like a living animal, fighting for its own life, even as the two trappers who clung desperately to the parting ropes fought to hold onto theirs. The struggle was never-ending. For mile after mile the leaping river, bloated from the spring snowmelt, drove them on. Cataract followed cataract, and after each one the raft would wobble like a skeleton. Finally, after one headlong plunge, the raft emerged leaving three of its logs racing separately alongside it.

Ropes began to snap like overtightened fiddle strings. Icy water sapped the men's strength, and Kit and Mark had no energy left to speak. All they could do was clench their teeth against the jarring dips and stomach-tingling rises, and pray that the raft would hold together long enough to reach a stretch of still water . . . if such a thing even existed in this canyon. Kit knew how some had come to call this stretch of the Green River "Hell's Canyon"; they had been swept away by it and lived to tell of the terror, and that at least gave him hope that the wild ride would eventually end.

Then suddenly the bouncing stopped. When Kit raised his head to look, the surface of the river appeared glass smooth, with that odd, green luminosity like a hundred deep fires churning beneath it. The water here must have been immensely deep, for nowhere was the surface rippled from unseen boulders below. Yet the water was still speeding along, if the passing shoreline was any indication.

Kit noted that half the raft had been torn away, and the few remaining logs were so detached from one another that huge gaps had opened in them. And through these gaps Kit's eyes were drawn to the odd green water beneath. Where did the light come from? The walls of the canyon rose thousands of feet to obscure the heavens. Only a thin blue slice of sky was visible. Yet somehow, through some quirk of nature, the water fairly glowed—or was it only his imagination?

The unnatural calm was like midnight in a graveyard, and for a brief heartbeat Kit had the same weightless sensation he'd had the day before, peering at this wild river from the cliffs which now stood two thousand feet overhead. Perhaps it had been this very spot he had been looking at. Then all at once the ghostly peace was shattered.

"Kit! Look at that!"

Mark's sudden panicky voice riveted Kit's attention as if it had been a Blackfoot war whoop. Mark was pointing up the river, and as Kit's eyes shot ahead, his heart leaped into his throat. "Now! We gotta jump *now*, Mark!"

"I can't!" Mark's fist was welded to the rope, as immovable as iron fastened there by the heat of a smithy's furnace. "You go, Kit! Save yourself if you can!"

The calm water ended in a funnel that shot through the narrows with the ferocity of a dozen erupting volcanoes. Kit's glance leaped from it to the quickly disappearing shoreline. Then he wrapped a rope around his arm, took a tight grip with his other hand, and squeezed his eyes shut.

The bottom dropped out of the river. A spire of rock shot up, shattering the raft. A cold hand pressed them deep beneath tons of foaming water and held them there. Kit's lungs began to ache, burning for a single gulp of air. But the river pressed him down, and tumbled him along until it was impossible to know in which direction lay air, and in which the rocky tomb. And when he thought his lungs had to explode, the river spat him out, only to dash him again upon the next staircase of roaring cataracts.

On and on went the beating, but somehow through the ordeal Kit kept his grip on the plunging logs, which by this time were all but scattered across the river. And somehow Mark had managed to hold on too. Kit was aware of this only in bits and pieces; for most of the ride he was either whirling underwater or shooting skyward. Then it happened. The shattered raft was violently sucked down into the icy depths, then vomited up again . . . and Mark was gone.

Through the blinding spray, Kit spied Mark's face bobbing to the surface; then his friend was sucked down. Instinctively, Kit marked the spot and dove down. The river instantly snatched him up, cast him to the bottom, battered him among the submerged rocks, and then kicked him out again—just another piece of debris in this mighty torrent! But somehow through it all, Kit had managed to grab a fistful of Mark's buckskin shirt, and once Kit's fingers closed about it, nothing, not even this wild water's vindictiveness, was going to tear them loose.

If the river wanted to have Mark, it was going to have to fight Kit Carson for the pleasure.

"See to them horses!" Joe Meek shouted, throwing off his hunting bag and powder horn as he dashed down the rocky beach. Casting caution to the wind, Joe sprang off a sandstone shelf and dove

23

into the water. A half-a-hundred powerful strokes put him on course, and then he had an arm around Jim Bridger. Bridger was having trouble in the powerful currents. The arrowhead buried deep in his back sometimes pressed a nerve and made his side go numb. Everyone knew of the wound, but there was not one of them confident enough to take a knife to Jim's back and cut the thing out.

Meek pulled Bridger to the shore, then immediately lent a hand to bring the horses safely to ground. Bridger recovered at once . . . and as he stood he saw the now-distant raft shudder against the first of the cataracts, then sweep swiftly out of sight beyond the gates of that hellish canyon.

"At least we didn't lose any of the horses, gov'ner," Swingle said in his clipped British accent, coming across the rocky beach, slinging river water from the sleeve of his shirt.

"No. Instead we lost two good men."

Meek brought the horses to picket. When he came back Bridger was already organizing a rescue party.

Klemper looked doubtful. "I've seen that canyon up close a time or two, Gabe. It's not likely that raft would hold together very long."

"I have seen it too," Gray Feather said, "and my people avoid it. Some claim it is haunted with the spirits of the Ancient Ones. But regardless of that, we have to at least make a search."

"I agree with Gray Feather," Newell added. "We have to make a search."

"Making a search was never in question," Bridger replied, asserting his authority as Booshway over these men. "Now, Gray Feather and me, we'll go back across to the other side and work our way up the west bank. Newell and Meek, you two go along

24

this east shore. While we're away, Swingle and Klemper will keep an eye on our gear."

Meek glanced down the river. "Ain't much of a shoreline, Gabe."

"Do your best, Joe." He frowned as he studied the towering chasm that lay before them. "It might be we'll have to climb that thing again once the bank ends."

"It might be we're just wasting time," Meek observed, eyeing with apprehension the nearly impenetrable obstacle that lay before them.

The jagged slit of glaring light overhead burned through a rent in the heavens . . . and lying there, Kit was suddenly staring into the blinding face of the Almighty.

His back ached mightily and his arm throbbed with a dull pain from a recently healed bullet wound in his shoulder that he had suffered that winter. It hadn't hurt for weeks, but now it burned like a lump of glowing coal buried deep beneath the healed-over flesh.

If this was Heaven, why hadn't he left the "vale of tears" behind the way all the hymns promised? If this was Heaven, why did he hurt so damn fiercely? If this was Heaven . . . or was it the other place?

That thought wrenched Kit from his half-dazed state, and a wave of relief swept over him. What he had taken for a rent in Heaven turned out to be, upon closer examination, the high, running slit of the canyon's walls, two thousand feet above, against the sky. And the face of the Almighty? It was really the sun standing straight overhead and casting its hot light against the naked rocks all around him.

Kit sat up painfully, and discovered his fist still clutched Mark's buckskin shirt.

"Mark!" He looked over his unconscious friend, finding nothing broken, but discovering a huge bruise upon his temple and his hair matted with dried blood. Kit had no idea how long they had lain there unconscious. It must have been hours, judging by the sun and the fact that their clothes were practically dry.

Kit stood stiffly and surveyed the small rocky beach upon which the Green River, after apparently deciding that Kit was a bitter pill to swallow, had spit them out. Nearby a small stream trickled from a narrow side canyon that meandered back to the west and disappeared into deep shadows. The beach was littered with driftwood, some stuffed into the cracks and crevices more than twenty feet over Kit's head. To the north, the river roared down a steep canyon, and a few hundred feet to the south, it took a plunge through another. Right here, however, the water merely rolled swiftly past with no breaking rapids. Just the same, they were trapped. There could be no escape either up or down the river short of resuming the wild ride, and Kit was in no market for that sort of excitement anytime soon.

Kit carried Mark into the shade of the side canyon and gathered driftwood for a fire. With flint and steel he started a small flame, and afterwards took inventory. He still had his tomahawk, butcher knife, awl, needles and thread, his patch knife, a pouch of bear grease, another pouch of bullets, which also held his straight razor, and a tin of caps that had been sealed with tallow and were dry. But when he shook his powder horn, water sloshed in-

26

side it. Well, little did that matter now, he thought wryly. They had lost their rifles.

His pipe had survived the calamity, but unfortunately his tobacco was soggy—and he could have used a smoke right about then. The sun had drifted farther to the west, no longer burning down upon them and turning the canyon into an oven. Kit checked Mark again, peered into his blank, dilated pupils, and felt for a pulse. The man was still out cold, but his breathing was steady and strong.

They were going to need food soon whether Kit could find a way out or not. He glanced into the narrow gash in the canyon's wall where the small stream issued. That way held possibilities, but with Mark still unconscious, Kit didn't want to stray too far and have his friend wake up while he was away. This beach covered about half an acre of rugged land that appeared completely cut off from the rest of the world. Down along the roaring river a narrow passage disappeared around a buttress of rock. Well, Kit thought, it was a place to start.

The way took him over the rushing torrents. A slip of the foot and there'd be no fighting his way free this time. Here the water shot down a series of roaring rapids, through a pinch in the canyon's walls. Kit recalled the words of the poem Gray Feather had recited: *All at once and all o'er, with a mighty uproar . . . And this way the Water comes down . . . at Lodore.*

Kit gave a wry grin. It was almost as if that Southey fellow was writing about this hellish place. He started onto the passage around the buttress of rock. It deposited him upon a second beach only a few dozen feet in width, but it was about five hundred feet long before a second outcropping brought it to an abrupt halt. There was enough driftwood here to keep a fire going for months, but without food . . . Well, there had to be food, even it was only the size of crows and rats.

Limping down the rocky shore, Kit imagined himself the only man left in the world, a world where the roar of the river drowned out even the crunch of his footsteps.

He let his gaze travel up the endless canyon walls. Perhaps they were climbable, but that would be an act of last resort. A hawk wheeled overhead as if keeping watch over this intruder into its world. That at least was a promising sign. Only one thing would bring a hawk down here, and that was food.

Ahead, Kit spied a pile of logs washed up and jammed into a gap between two rocks. As he drew nearer, he saw that some of the logs were remnants of the raft. Nearer still, Kit realized that one of the logs held their rifles, still lashed tight to it. The sight lifted his spirits almost as much as if he'd discovered a ladder out of this hellish canyon.

Taking care, he climbed the unsteady mass and worked his way in among the bramble of flotsam. Taking a precarious perch, Kit loosened the knots and carried the rescued rifles up onto the bank. He went back for the rope, and spent nearly half an hour retrieving as much of it as he could. Rope might prove to be even more valuable than the rifles—at least right now with their powder wet.

Taking up the prizes, Kit returned to the first beach where he had left Mark. His spirits had lifted several notches, and he was anxious for Mark to come to so they could begin making plans. Coming back around the outcropping of rock, Kit leaped lightly to the beach and stopped sharply.

At least twenty armed Indians stood around his unconscious partner . . . and they spotted him at that same instant.

Chapter Three

In a glance Kit measured up the situation. There was only one place these warriors could have come from: the narrow side canyon. That meant there was a way out of this gorge. But little good it would do him and Mark with their scalps dangling from a war lance. Kit's jaw took a determined set as he leveled both rifles and drew back the hammers.

True, the powder was soaked and the weapons useless for anything but bashing in a few skulls, but the Indians didn't have to know that.

"Back off, bucks!" Kit growled, taking a menacing step forward, but he might as well have spoken to the rocky walls for all the response he got. It occurred to him that these men didn't understand English. It also became clear to Kit as he stalked nearer and they moved apart, presenting the points of their spears, that they were unlike any tribe he had ever encountered in this great western wilderness.

"I've the teeth of a grizzly b'ar and the claws of the panther. Stand clear of that man unless you want to reap the wrath of a whirlwind!" Kit boasted in Spanish, looking for some response.

Nothing.

Kit drew up, for once stymied. "All right, what language *do* you *hombres* talk? 'Rapaho? Crow? Shian?"

They didn't answer that, but to Kit's relief, they didn't immediately attack either. They just stood there looking at him, and he at them. Kit couldn't tell who was more amazed at the encounter, and he had a feeling that these Indians were trying to sort things out too. He had either met or heard stories of just about every tribe known to the white trappers, but never had he seen or heard of any Indians like these men. "You ain't Eutahs, I can tell that," he said in the tongue of his friend Gray Feather.

A warrior spoke, coming forward a step to face Kit. His language was one Kit had never heard, but curiously enough, it vaguely resembled a dialect of Tiwa that he had learned from the Indians that lived in the Taos Pueblo. But that was impossible. There were no Pueblo Indians this far north.

Kit lowered the rifles. "We are friends," he said, drawing on his limited knowledge of Tiwa.

"Friends?" The man, whom Kit judged to be their leader, used a different word, but it was mighty close to the phrase Kit had employed. "From where come?"

Kit pointed up the river. Immediately there arose a heated debate among the other warriors. The leader threw up a hand, silencing them. This man was taller than the others, but still on the short side at about five feet three inches. He was powerfully built, and his long, black hair hung down to the middle of his back, bound together in a leather band and decorated with the tail feather of a red hawk. He carried a spear, and wore a flint knife in his belt. Some of the men, Kit noted, were armed with bows and arrows, and some just carried spears tipped with long, shaped-flint points. A few of the men held an odd weapon that Kit didn't recognize: a long paddlelike contraption with a short arrow nocked in it.

"You come from Seguro's sleep world, the place of the dead?" the leader asked with concern in his voice.

Kit grinned after sorting that out. "No, I come from the living, but for a while thar I sure thought I was gonna be dead."

The man tentatively touched the sleeve of Kit's shirt, as if to reassure himself that Kit was not a ghost. When he discovered solid flesh and muscle beneath it, everyone seemed to relax. At no time did these warriors make a threatening move towards Kit or the unconscious trapper at their naked feet. Just the same, the way they held their weapons spoke clearly of their willingness to use them if need be.

"Me Stone Claw," the leader said, thumping his breast; then he dropped a hand to the flint knife at his side as if the weapon was somehow related to his moniker.

"My name is Christopher Carson, but folks generally just call me Kit. We seem to be stuck here, and my partner took a knock to his head and is in a bad way. I'd be obliged if you could show us the way out of this canyon."

It took a couple of rephrasings and a lot of sign language to get that idea across to Stone Claw, but once he understood he shot some orders to the men with him, and at once six of the sturdy warriors hefted Mark onto their shoulders and started into the shadowy slit in the canyon's wall. For a while they walked through the stream; then the slit widened out and suddenly the Indians started up the sheer wall, clinging to it like a spider on a thread. Kit caught his breath seeing Mark being borne along up the nearly vertical rock face. But these men moved with the surefootedness of a mountain goat.

Stone Claw waited with Kit at the base of the wall as his men made the ascent. When they reached a ledge, Stone Claw motioned for Kit to go next. Carved into the face of the canyon wall were toe- and handholds, their edges worn smooth from what must have been many years of use. Kit let his gaze travel up the towering rock wall, grimaced, then slung the two buffalo guns across his back and started up.

Where these Indians fairly flew up the side, even burdened as they had been by the unconscious man, Kit's progress was slow and methodical, each shift of hand and foot carefully made. Stone Claw must have been impatient with the white trapper as he followed along behind him. But if he was, he kept it to himself and let Kit make the ascent at his own pace.

Finally reaching the trail, Kit drew in a long breath and took a peek at the dizzying depth from which he had climbed. Stone Claw urged him on, and Kit tried not to think of the narrowness of the trace as he resumed the trek up the vertical canyon wall.

Ghosts of Lodore

*   *   *

They had picked up the stream again, and in a little while entered a canyon that was perhaps three hundred feet wide. Here a small band of men chopped at the ground with stone tools, cutting long furrows into it. Nearby, some women were clearing irrigation ditches where water diverted from the stream entered the furrows. In another section of the small canyon, a field of newly plowed ground was already showing bright green where shoots of recently planted crops had begun to push their heads up through the earth.

Everyone ceased in their labors to watch this small company march by. Kit felt the probing curiosity of each pair of dark eyes upon him.

"Your people?" he asked Stone Claw.

The stoic warrior nodded, and with the spear he pointed ahead. "My village."

Kit turned to look. What he saw brought him instantly to a halt. Halfway up the canyon wall was a wide shelf of rock, and upon this stood a stone enclosure of at least fifty lodges, some built right on top of the ones below, each with a small window, and a doorway nearly as tiny. Crude wooden ladders climbed from one story to the next, and Indians ascended and descended these with startling nimbleness, some even while balancing baskets upon their heads.

The lowering sun reflected off these stone cliff houses, which shone as if they had been built of burnished bronze. Kit began walking again, but his eyes remained fixed upon the cliff village. Never had he seen anything like this in all of his travels.

"Stone Claw, what are your people called?"

The chief gave him a blank look. "Called? I do not understand."

"Do your people have a name? What is your tribe?"

He caught the drift of Kit's question. "We are—" Here he spoke a word which, as near as Kit could translate, worked out to be *Children from inside the Earth*.

The men carried Mark up into the cliff village and, at Stone Claw's orders, into one of the little rock houses perched as precariously as a swallow's nest. Stooping through the low doorway, Kit found himself in a small room. At the rear was another small door, and beyond it he saw movement, and the flicker of firelight upon the dark walls.

A woman emerged from the shadowy depths of that back room as Stone Claw was directing his men to lay Mark upon a sleeping pallet of woven strips of saplings that was covered in a blanket of deerskin. The woman was startled at first at seeing the white trapper. Her gaze leaped from Mark to Kit, then to Stone Claw for an explanation. As he was giving it, a second face emerged from the shadows of the back room.

She was a pretty girl of maybe sixteen, with wide, curious eyes. She wore her hair in twin braids, each encased in a leather cuff halfway down their length. Her doeskin dress was decorated with colored porcupine quills and little dangling charms made of something Kit could not identify in the poor light. She was just about the prettiest Indian girl Kit had ever seen, and he'd seen plenty of right pretty native women in his day.

Their eyes met, and Kit smiled at her. To his delight, she returned the smile, and seemed not the least anxious to avert her eyes. Suddenly one of the young warriors who had brought Mark up here stepped between them, and his narrowed scowl was anything but friendly, Kit decided. The look of jealousy was the same in every language, in every culture. Giving him a wry grin, Kit returned his attention to Mark. The older woman was examining the bloodied scab on the trapper's skull, speaking too quickly for Kit to follow. But her words carried authority, and at once a couple of the men sprang from the cramped quarters to do her bidding.

Kit was only in the way here, for the woman—Stone Claw's wife, he surmised—had the situation well in hand. Kit stepped outside and watched the people in the valley below, small and insectlike from high up on the cliff. Falls and the injuries falls caused were probably well known to these people who lived in lodges perched halfway up the side of a sheer cliff, and Kit was certain that Mark was in good hands.

Shadows lengthened across the valley as the field workers were making their way home, scurrying up the rickety ladders and disappearing into the tiny doorways. The returning workers made a wide detour around Kit, giving him quick, guarded looks, then quietly talking among themselves. Some went up to the roof of this massive many-roomed building, and then down the other side, just to avoid coming too near him.

He marveled at the stone architecture that seemed to defy gravity in places. It reminded him a little of the Taos Pueblo, but was of a much cruder nature. Still, the similarity was striking. If this place had been built on flat ground instead of halfway up the side of a canyon wall . . . if it had been built of adobe bricks instead of native stone . . . if—

Suddenly the hairs at the nape of Kit's neck lifted.

Someone had stepped quietly up behind him. With catlike reflexes, Kit whirled around.

The girl from inside Stone Claw's lodge, who had earlier caught his eye, drew in a sudden gasp. The swiftness of his movements startled her. She took an involuntary step backwards, misjudged her location upon the high, narrow walkway, and as her foot stabbed back into the nothingness of open space, she teetered there a moment on the brink of a hundred-foot drop, her arms clawing frantically at the air, then fell. . . .

Chapter Four

Kit shot out an arm and caught her about the waist an instant before she had completely lost her balance, snatching her from the jaws of certain death. As he reeled her back, using his momentum to keep them both from pitching over the edge, she frantically threw a pair of strong arms around the trapper, nearly squeezing the breath from him. In spite of having just narrowly averted a disaster, he found the arrangement rather pleasant. Whether out of fright, or out of a similar feeling, the pretty girl remained in his arms some moments longer than absolutely necessary under the circumstances—until a voice behind them barked out a sharp word.

Kit turned as the girl instantly broke off the embrace. The same young warrior who had intervened earlier was standing there, his burning glare fixed upon Kit. His hand moved toward the flint knife thrust in the band of his breechclout. "Get away from the stranger," he ordered her.

With eyes averted, she slipped past Kit and quickly ducked back through the small door. The man watched her until she had disappeared. His dark eyes shifted back to Kit.

With Mark still unconscious and at the mercy of these people, Kit didn't want to antagonize anyone. This fellow obviously had misread his intentions, and the mountain man was about to set the fellow straight about what had happened when the long sliver of flint came from the Indian's waistband.

"I have heard the old legends of men with skin white like bones and hair on faces. All stories come to bad end. It is said that Father Moon marked some men in such a way so that we would know them, and be wary of their evil."

Kit was getting a handle on this primitive dialect of Tiwa, and he knew he had just been insulted! Precarious situation or not, he was of a mind to lay into the brash young man and scatter his bravado all over this pile of stones. But he refrained, hearing Jim Bridger's warning voice in his head. Bridger had been in the mountains longer than most men, and he'd learned from hard experience that going off half cocked was the surest way to end up buried in these mountains. Kit had a tendency to act first and think about it later, but he learned quickly.

Grinning, Kit swallowed bile and said easily, "The gal stumbled and I only kept her from falling. Put that knife away before you cut someone with it."

"Night-Sky Feather is promised to me. She is to be my woman. No man is permitted to put a hand on her. It is my right to defend what is mine."

"I'm not tryin' to take what is yours, buck. Let's

drop it before *you* get hurt." Kit had wanted to say "someone" instead of "you," but his hackles were getting up. It had all been an accident, after all. And he *had* saved her life, hadn't he? If anything the fellow should have been shaking Kit's hand and buying him a drink—or whatever the equivalent was among these people.

But the subtle insult hadn't been lost on the Indian. His glowering dark eyes narrowed, and Kit saw the muscles grow taut—like the thews of a mountain lion preparing to spring upon an unsuspecting rabbit. Well, he had tried to do it Jim's way and that hadn't worked. Now he'd have to do it his own way. Kit slipped his wide butcher knife from its leather sheath, the lowering sunlight glinting red along its polished steel blade.

The warrior had rocked forward onto the balls of his feet, but all of a sudden he froze as his narrowed eyes widened more than just a little and fixed upon the knife in Kit's hand . . . as if he'd never seen such a thing.

For an instant Kit didn't know which way it would go. Then a man's voice called out.

"Bone Breaker! What is this about?"

The warrior—Bone Breaker—backed off a step and turned. An old man stood upon the narrow path that ran the length of stone lodges at this level, connecting each one to the other. He was dressed in a cloak made from braided strips of rabbit skin. The garment dropped nearly to the man's naked toes. Around his neck was a string of bones—the vertebrae from some animal, Kit surmised, although which animal was a mystery to him. Perhaps it was from the same dog whose sightless eye sockets and gaping teeth now topped the staff the old man held firmly in his right hand. His long black hair was decorated with bits of bird bones, and a tattoo, like the coils of a snake, began as a spiral around his left breast and climbed up his neck, where the snake's head came to rest upon the man's dark cheek, just below the left eye.

All and all, he was the strangest-looking critter Kit could recall ever seeing. But when he spoke, there was the ring of authority in his still-strong voice.

"I ask you again. Why do you show anger to this stranger who has come into our midst?"

Bone Breaker said, "Ghost Talker, you of anyone here should know why. Nothing is hidden from your eyes. This stranger has the white skin that the ancient legends have warned us about. He touched Night-Sky Feather. It is my right to defend what will soon be mine."

The old man leaned upon the staff, his stare a piercing arrow that impaled the young warrior. "It is true, nothing is hidden from these eyes." A gnarled finger tapped the snake's head tattooed upon his cheek. "Too bad that young men, with eyes that still see clear and far, cannot also see what is up close and true."

"I do not understand, Ghost Talker."

"No, you would not. The ears do not hear and the eyes do not see in young men in whom blood still boils. But Ghost Talker sees. The truth is that Night-Sky Feather had slipped, and had fallen into the arms of Seguro, but this white-skinned man with the color of sky in his eyes reached out and fought Seguro, and pulled her back from the river where our ancestors have gone."

At the sound of the commotion Stone Claw and the other warriors had emerged from the little stone lodge. They were listening to the old man's words. Night-Sky Feather was there too. Stone

Claw put a fatherly arm about the girl's shoulder, as if to shield her from any further harm.

"I did not know this," Bone Breaker said with sudden despair in his voice. Bone Breaker stared a moment at the old man, then gave Night-Sky Feather a desperate look—one that Kit had only seen a time or two before—on the faces of those who had gathered at the local cemetery for a final farewell. He turned suddenly away from them and fairly flew down one of the slick ladders. A moment later Kit caught a glimpse of the man hurrying away down the valley; then Bone Breaker disappeared behind a shoulder of rock.

When Kit finally looked back at the people gathered there, they were studying him oddly. He didn't know what it meant, and he gave a quick grin. "Whal, reckon we can be happy nothin' came of that, heh?"

But no one there was smiling . . . no one, that is, except Night-Sky Feather.

Kit's mouth went dry, and his moccasins suddenly seemed too tight. He had a bad feeling about this, but before he could sort out what their looks meant, a low groan emerged from the rock lodge. A moment later Stone Claw's wife stuck her head outside and said, "The stranger is awake."

"This child figured he'd gone to beaver for a certain, Kit," Mark said weakly. "Never thought I'd be opening my eyes on this side of eternity again."

Kit gave a short laugh. "That river counted coups on us, Mark, but it missed the long shot. Just the same, I'm in no hurry to go up again' her anytime soon."

Mark momentarily closed his eyes, running a tongue over his cracked lips. Then he looked

41

around, taking in the small room and the faces bent over Kit's shoulders, looking down at him. "Where am I?"

"Don't rightly know for sure where we are. We were stuck down at the bottom of the canyon when these folks showed up. They seem friendly enough . . . at least most of 'em do. They carried you up from the river and into this side canyon. It was a mighty fierce climb, and you're lucky you had your eyes closed. The way I judge it, we're nearly at the top of the plateau."

Mark managed a grin; then his gaze went around the crowd, studying the faces that looked back at him. "What tribe?"

"Haven't ciphered that one out yet."

"They look a little like Diggers."

"I thought so too at first, but they ain't. They ain't like no Injun I've ever met. Talk a sort of Tiwa lingo, but with lots of words missing, and a few new ones I've never heard before added in."

"Tiwa? This far north?"

Kit shrugged. "Like I said, I ain't figured it out yet, Mark. They call themselves the Children from inside the Earth."

He closed his eyes again. "Feels like a buffler walked all over me, Kit."

"I know what you mean."

Stone Claw's wife, an attractive woman whose name, Kit had learned, was After Snow Rain, knelt beside Mark and gently lifted his head, putting a gourd to his lips. Mark took a sip. His mouth screwed up and he pushed the gourd aside, but Mrs. Stone Claw was insistent, and in the end Mark took most of the foul liquid.

"It tastes like buffler piss!"

Kit laughed. "She knows what's best for you. I

reckon these people are right familiar with folks falling and hitting their heads."

"What do you mean?"

"Once you're well enough to walk around some and take a gander at this place you'll know what I'm saying. Meanwhile, you just stay still and heal up some. I have a feeling we'll have a tall climb and a long walk before we catch up with Gabe and the boys."

Kit stepped back outside onto the terrace that stretched along the front of Stone Claw's lodge, connecting it with other lodges along the cliff. The valley far below lay in deep shadows now; the last glow of daylight was quickly fading from the sky. All along the canyon the cliff sides were dotted with small fires, and in many of the tiny windows was the flickering glow of firelight within. Oddly enough, Kit noted as he studied the pueblo-like lodges built on the cliffs, a large number of lodges were dark, as if uninhabited. Almost as if at one time this village had contained many more people than it did now.

The air was sweet with the fragrance of spring, and there was a pleasant odor of moisture rising from the ground. This little valley seemed fertile, and these people had worked the land well, taking advantage of the little stream that coursed through the center of it. As he thought it over, it was easy to see how this small tribe might have been over-looked by the white trappers, and that would explain the surprise he had seen in Bone Breaker's eyes when Kit had pulled his butcher knife. Bone Breaker had probably never seen a steel blade before. Perhaps no one in this village had seen steel before. Kit had detected no steel arrowheads among any of the warriors, and that was usually the first item of trade a tribe acquired when it met up with the white man.

The villagers seemed happy enough with their lives, yet Kit sensed an underlying tension in this valley. He felt the uneasiness in the stares that he got from these people, and in the wide berth that most of the cliff people so far had given him. Was it because he and Mark had shown up? Was that what was making them wary? Had they so seldom seen strangers? Or was there something else going on?

"Kit." Night-Sky Feather's lyrical voice brought Kit from his reverie. He turned and found her standing upon the terrace pathway, with only a few feet separating them.

"Ma'am," Kit said respectfully. Considering all the fuss folks hereabouts made when strangers got too cozy with their womenfolk, he intended to keep his distance. His only thoughts were to get himself and Mark safely on their way as soon as possible . . . regardless of the unsettling fact that Night-Sky Feather's wide, inquiring eyes, her perky, oval face, and pleasing smile were making his heart beat a bit faster than normal.

She came a step closer, tentatively. Then all at once the lovely Indian girl threw herself into his arms, clutching Kit about the waist with all her strength and pressing her cheek hard to his chest.

"Ma'am!" he yelped, startled. "What are you doing?" Try as he might, Kit could not break her grip short of harming the girl.

Just then Stone Claw stuck his head out the door to see what was going on, and Kit knew his hopes for a peaceable departure from this strange village were doomed.

Confounded women! They always seemed to get romance in their heads at the worse possible times!

Chapter Five

To Kit's utter amazement, Stone Claw merely grinned and pulled his head back inside.

Kit managed to break Night-Sky Feather's grip on him. "What was that for?" he asked.

"To show my new husband that I will be a good wife."

"Husband! When did this all happen?"

"When you took me back form Seguro's sleep world where the ghosts of the ancestors live."

Kit gulped hard, his thoughts suddenly jumbled and tripping over one another. "Hold up thar, Night-Sky Feather. This is all news to me. What about Bone Breaker? Ain't he pledged to be your husband?"

"He was, but your deed has given me to you."

"Wagh! I think we need to talk about this some, ma'am. You see, soon as my partner is fit to travel, him and me are skedaddling outa here. We're due at the Rendezvous next month with Bridger and the others."

"Then I will go with you."

"Now . . . now that might not work out too good, ma'am. See, I'm not certain I'm ready to take on a wife just yet. I ain't hardly got enough money to buy all them foofuraws that a squaw needs to feel proper among the other Injun women at Rendezvous."

"I do not understand all this that you say, but you can teach?"

"Err, whal, if the truth be known, I ain't much of a schoolmaster, ma'am." The terrace seemed suddenly crowded, and Kit was not of a mind to debate her right there on the doorstep to her lodge with so many folks looking on. "Reckon thar's someplace we can go and talk this over?"

She took his hand, and the next moment Kit found himself edging along a narrow foothold snaking up the side of the cliff that towered above the stone lodges. Night-Sky Feather moved with the surefootedness of an ant, but Kit had difficulty, not helped any by the lump in his throat when he looked past the tips of his moccasins into the shadowy depths of the valley at least ten thousand feet down! Well, maybe not quite that deep, but it might just as well have been, considering his precarious perch way up there. Then the ledge opened up on the top of the cliffs. It was the high plateau, probably not too far from where a few days before he and the others had stopped to look at the river far below.

Kit found a low, flat rock to sit upon and he anchored himself there, grateful for something solid beneath him. This cliff living might be all right for billy goats, mountain lions, and these cliff-dwelling

Indians, but it didn't suit Kit in the least.

"What do you want to talk about," she asked, her big, liquid eyes peering deep into his, her closeness most unsettling. That they were completely alone up here, and in the dark, didn't help matters any either.

"I'm not sure you really want to hitch your cart onto my team, ma'am."

"What is 'cart'?"

"Whal, what I mean to say is, I kinda move around a lot. I get the feeling that you and your people don't stray far from this valley. I don't think you'd like leaving your family and friends."

"You can stay here."

"Oh, no, I don't think that would work either."

Night-Sky Feather seemed not to be listening to his objections, her thoughts off somewhere else. "Where is your village?"

"Wherever I throw down my blanket, I reckon. But if you mean where did I come from, whal, my kinfolk live back east, in a place called Missouri."

"Is it far beyond the canyon's rim?"

"I reckon it's more 'n a thousand miles beyond it."

"I do not understand. How far is that?"

Kit rolled his shoulders. "It might take a man fifty or sixty passages of your Father Moon to walk such a distance."

This was clearly something she could not comprehend, and she changed subjects. "What does your name mean?"

"Kit? Why, that's just a short handle for Christopher is all. Reckon I don't know exactly what Christopher means. I never give it much thought. Just sorta always used it natural-like. Ain't no special meaning to it. Not like Injuns put meaning to names. Take your name for instance, Night-Sky Feather. I'll wager a pack of plews to a pint of Dupont that there's a special meaning to it."

She smiled and pointed at the night sky, her arm tracing an arc across it. "That is the Night-Sky Feather."

Kit grinned. "Reckon it do look a little like a feather away up thar. My people call it the Milky Way."

"Milky Way? It sounds funny. What does it mean?"

Kit laughed. "My, you're just full of questions. Does everything have to have a meaning to it?"

She blinked. "Everything does have a meaning," she said flatly, and Kit reckoned that was true . . . in her world.

"You know, I think I better get back down and check up on my partner." He stood, but she was determined to have him a little longer to herself.

"Tell me more," she insisted.

Kit gave a slight grin. "You tell me something, Night-Sky Feather. What is it about your people that's making them as jittery as a sinner in the front pew? Is it Mark and me?"

She frowned. "It is not that." Her voice grew suddenly sober. "It is the Enemy from Above. They came a few days ago and killed many of the People. They have attacked our village three times since the snow has gone. They are strong, and many. We used to be many, but no more. Ghost Talker speaks now of the Ancient Ones, and tells the People they will soon have to leave this place and go to the place of the Ancient Ones. His visions have made the People unhappy. No one wants to leave. There is never a time in the old stories when the People have not lived here, in the center of Mother Earth."

"Hum, so that's it. Some tribe has found you out and are making raids."

"They are fearsome warriors. They come from the west to steal our food, and kill the People."

"Sound like Diggers to me."

"I do not know that name."

"The Pau-Eutaw. A mangy band of ill-fed, ill-tempered critters. We just call 'em Diggers, and keep outta their way when we can." Kit stood again. "I reckon I better go and see how Mark is doing."

Her playful smile had vanished when she told of the attacks, and now she did not try to stop him. Kit took a step towards the rim of the canyon and the narrow ledge down to the cliff lodges. Suddenly he heard a footstep behind him. He turned, and at that same instant Night-Sky Feather gave a startled scream. Something swung out of the blackness of the night at his head. Kit threw up an arm in time to cushion the blow, and the next moment he was sprawled upon the still-warm rock, unable to move. Before his vision went completely out of focus and the cold hand of unconsciousness closed around him, he was vaguely aware of the struggle going on nearby. He heard Night-Sky Feather scream a second time . . . and then black nothingness enveloped him.

The odor of wood smoke filled his senses at first, and then slowly the stream of sunlight broke through the blackness and stabbed into his eyes. Kit lay absolutely still, listening, trying to determine the enemy's strength before giving himself away. All he heard, however, was the soft, rhythmic breathing of someone nearby. Kit parted an eye ever so slightly. He was back in Stone Claw's lodge!

He sat up. Across the way Mark stirred and

looked over. "Ain't we a pair, Kit," he said. "You'd figure two growed-up men would have a better use for their noggins than to stop rocks."

Kit fingered the lump on the back of his head. "What happened?" Then he remembered. "Night-Sky Feather!"

"She was here a while ago, checking up on you."

"She's all right?"

"Appeared so."

"What happened?"

Mark sat up too and said, "It seems you've got a jealous boyfriend on your hands, Kit. He tried to brain you, but that gal kept him off of you until her screams brought the men of this village to her rescue. I reckon she's a wildcat when she's protecting her man." Mark grinned and gave him a wink.

"You know, Mark, I think it's time we pack our possible bag and head out of here."

"Except we lost our possible bag in that river, remember?"

Kit frowned and stood. "You up to making a march?"

"I don't know." Mark tried to stand, swayed a moment, then shot out a hand and caught himself. Kit lowered his friend back to the pallet.

"I guess not," Kit said.

Mark said, "Looks like I'm marooned here a few more days at least. Anyway, what's your hurry, Kit? They caught that devil, Bone Breaker, and threw him into the brig. And that gal's really taken with you. I don't see why you're in such a hurry. We'll still make the Rendezvous in time."

That she was "taken with him" was reason enough. Kit was not like some men who glibly led a gal down the garden path only to leave her behind once their lusts were satisfied. No, when Kit decided to take a woman, it would be a serious commitment—a lifelong commitment. But he didn't tell Mark this. Such notions of propriety were generally frowned upon by men of the mountains, where the wild abandon of Indian women was an enticing alternative to the prim and proper women back East who eschewed showing even a bit of ankle, and whose lovemaking was generally done with the candle snuffed.

"Night-Sky Feather told me that thar's some kind of trouble brewing between them and some Diggers who've taken to making raids on this village," Kit said.

"Diggers? What do they want with these peaceful folks?" Mark asked.

Kit gave a short laugh. "What do them rascals generally want? They come to steal food and collect a scalp or two."

"What are you figuring to do about it, Kit?"

Kit hadn't thought that far ahead yet. "I don't know, Mark. I'm hoping we'll be away from here before any more trouble comes." As he said it, he was thinking about Stone Claw and After Snow Rain and their open hospitality. And he was thinking about Night-Sky Feather too. Diggers were the scourge of the desert region to the west, an unpredictable people who searched for food and seemed always on the move. These people who had befriended him and Mark were no match for the Diggers. Kit suspected it was only through the good fortune of their hidden location that they had survived this long. But that advantage, apparently, had somehow been lost.

Kit's head was throbbing when he stepped out into the morning sunlight. Below him the villagers were busy plowing and planting, gathering fire-wood and hauling water. Along the terrace walk a few dozen feet away two women were busy shaping a clay pot, happily chattering away. They momentarily stopped and looked at him, then resumed their work. Below, among the busy villagers, Kit spied Stone Claw and After Snow Rain coming up the trail that crossed the tilled valley. She carried a basket, and he a long pole over his shoulder with a large fish impaled upon its end. They glanced up and saw Kit at that same instant. Stone Claw handed the pole to his wife, and as she went off to join some other women, he scurried up the ladders, terrace to terrace, until his face appeared above the ladder near Kit's moccasins.

"Good you awake, Kit. Head hurt?"

"Not nearly as much as my pride. I should've never let that buck sneak up on me like he done. If it warn't for your daughter, I'd have gone under for sure." Kit saw in Stone Claw's blank look that he had missed most of that. Language was still a problem, but at least most of the time he was able to get his meaning across.

"Come," the chief said, quick-stepping his way back down the ladder. Kit followed at a slower pace. Down two terraces, then along a wide ledge of rock to a flat, paved area of the cliff village. Here was a rectangular opening in the pavement with the top of a ladder sticking up from the shadowy depths below. And here also stood an upright post, and tied to it was a rope.

The rope ran back into the shadows beneath the cliff where Bone Breaker was sitting. The young warrior stood and stepped out into the sunlight. The other end of the rope had been securely fastened around his wrists. He scowled at Kit and paced like a trapped animal.

Stone Claw said, "Bone Breaker has brought disgrace upon the People. We pledge safety to any visitor in our village. He has broken that pledge." The chief bent, took a large stone off the pavement, and handed it to Kit.

"What's this for?"

"It is your right to punish Bone Breaker in the same manner that he hurt you."

"Hum. In other words, an eye for an eye." Kit glanced at the stone, then dropped it. "I don't reckon I can blame him too much, Stone Claw. Heck, if I was smitten with a gal and another man come along and caught her eye, I might do the same as Bone Breaker thar."

"But it is your right."

"Whal, I reckon then it's my right just to forget about it, Stone Claw."

"What are you doing?"

Kit glanced from his work and grinned at Night-Sky Feather, who had just climbed to the terrace in front of her father's lodge, carrying a decorated clay pot filled with water.

"You have more questions than Betsy's got stitches," Kit replied. Earlier he had emptied his and Mark's powder horns onto a piece of rabbit skin and set the lumpy powder out to dry in the sunlight. "I'm breaking up the lumps and grinding it back into powder so it will go bang again."

"Bang?"

Kit pretended to hold his rifle and squeeze the trigger. "Bang!"

She laughed.

53

"You have no idea what I'm talkin' about, do you?"

Night-Sky Feather shook her head.

"Ever see one of these?" Kit took one of the rifles that he had earlier cleaned and oiled.

"It is a war club?" she asked, setting down the clay pot and taking the heavy piece by the barrel, cocking it over her shoulder.

"Not exactly, but it do got a wallop like you ain't never seen before." Kit took the rifle back, leaned it against the wall with the other one, and went back to gently crushing the hard grains of gunpowder beneath a river-rounded boulder. "Later I'll show you what they're for."

"Head hurt?" She gently touched the black-and-blue lump on his forehead.

"A horse kicked me once and that hurt a whole lot worse."

"Horse?"

"Like a big dog," he explained, knowing she'd understand that since the village seemed to have more than its share of mutts. But it only made matters worse. By her wondering expression Kit knew that she was trying to picture a dog kicking anyone. "Never mind, it ain't important."

A shuffling sound brought their heads around. Mark was just ducking under the doorway. He emerged unsteadily, leaned against the stone wall, and squinted in the bright sunlight. "I'm making progress, Kit. Another day or two and we can be on our way."

"I'm ready," Kit answered in English, looking at the pretty Indian girl. For the first time since their catastrophic arrival there, he wasn't sure he was so anxious to leave. Night-Sky Feather was growing on him. It felt good a moment ago to have a woman fussing over his well-being.

Mark looked around, seeing for the first time the rock buildings: some with square corners, others rounded like the turrets of some crude castle. "What is this place? Where the devil are we anyway?"

"I haven't got that worked out yet, Mark. Near as I can figure it, that river must've carried us a lot further than we reckoned."

"What do your mean?"

"When we was swept away it was 1835. Judging from these people—people who ain't even seen steel yet—who knows where we might have ended up? Why, I wouldn't be surprised to see Hannibal's elephants come marching down over them cliffs right this very instant."

Mark peered at him a moment, stunned, then laughed. "You're just joshing, I can tell."

Kit only grinned as he finished crushing the gunpowder.

Chapter Six

It wasn't exactly Hannibal's army, but so soon did it come on the heels of Kit's remark that the effect was nearly as startling. He had finished crushing the last of their black powder, and had just refilled the two powder horns, when a shrill yipping from a half-a-hundred throats rang down at them from the cliffs above them. In the next instant fifty dusky warriors were swarming over the rim and descending to the valley floor.

"Diggers!" Mark hissed. Night-Sky Feather let out a short startled cry.

Kit grabbed up their rifles and tossed one to Mark. They each spilled a measure of powder down the barrel, chased it with a patched ball, and fitted a cap to the nipple. Kit leaped to the ladder and scrambled down it. Above, Mark slipped to a sitting position with his elbows upon his knees, steadying his sights on one of the Diggers across the valley.

As Kit made his way toward the valley floor below he saw that Stone Claw was already organizing his warriors. Some of the women fled into the safety of the lower stone lodges, while others emerged with arms filled with the queer featherless arrows and the odd paddles that Kit had noticed upon first discovering Stone Claw's warriors.

By this time the first of the Diggers had reached the valley floor. A volley of arrows rained into the cliff warriors, glancing off stone walls, one or two finding their mark. Stone Claw's men returned the attack, and Kit had his first demonstration of how the paddle-weapons worked. Fitting a arrow into one, the warrior cocked the paddle over his shoulder then snapped it out, sending the arrow zinging towards its target.

A quaint form of warfare, Kit thought, but apparently aiming beyond a few yards was a problem, as most of the darts missed their targets. The men wielding bows and arrows had a little better luck . . . yet the odds were tilted decidedly toward the Diggers, who had more powerful bows and more skill in this sort of fighting. Stone Claw rallied his men and moved them toward the eastern canyon wall, where the descent was the easiest and the Diggers most numerous. The valley rang with howls and war whoops as two groups clashed; bows and arrows giving way to knives and spears.

Just then a rifle shot echoed through the valley, and across the way a Digger let out a yelp and fell from his purchase high up on the eastern wall. For an instant the reverberating thunder brought both parties to a halt. The cliff villagers seemed to be the more startled of the two groups. The respite lasted only a heartbeat. Then once again the war whoops filled the valley. Kit glanced up to see Mark running

57

another ball down the barrel of his Hawkens. Night-Sky Feather appeared as a dark granite statue, her back pressed against the stone wall of her father's lodge, her eyes locked in wide surprise upon the rifle which Mark was once again bringing to bear.

Movement to the west drew Kit's eye. A half-dozen Diggers had started down a cleft in the rock wall, apparently yet unnoticed by the cliff villagers fanning out to stop the steady flows of these enemies into their deep sanctuary. Kit threw his J. J. Henry to his shoulder and lining up the sights, touched the single trigger. The rifle barked and leaped in his hands. At the cleft one of the invading warriors clawed the air as the ground rushed up. The rifle shot this time had no effect on the fighting going on around him other than to momentarily turn a few heads. Kit quickly reloaded. Overhead Mark's rifle boomed again.

Kit rounded a corner of the stone lodges in time to see the paved plaza where Bone Breaker was still tied with a long rope to the post. At that moment two Digger warriors dropped from above. Bone Breaker leaped, driving a heel into the throat of one of the Diggers. The other Digger, momentarily startled by this unexpected attack, quickly recovered and, fitting an arrow to his bow, took aim and drew back. . . .

The heavy ball from Kit's buffalo gun shattered the man's brisket and flipped him over the edge of the terrace to the ground more than twenty feet below. Kit charged up a ladder to the first terrace and along the pathway to where Bone Breaker was finishing off the first Digger with a heavy boulder. Bone Breaker glanced up, wild-eyed, as Kit wheeled to a halt.

"You'd be a mite more useful down fightin' at Stone Claw's side than up here taking on the Diggers with your hands tied," Kit said, drawing the glinting steal blade from its sheath. Bone Breaker thrust out his hands, and in an instant Kit had severed the leather thongs that bound them. All at once Kit threw himself into the young warrior and as his weight carried them both back into the wall, a war lance glanced off the flat paving where a moment before they had been standing.

Rolling to his feet, Kit cocked the butcher knife over his shoulder and flung it at the man descending the cliff from above. The man's scream filled the plaza between the tall lodges, and then his body broke on the paving stones at Kit's feet. Kit freed the knife from the man's back as Bone Breaker appropriated his bow and quiver of arrows. With a yelp of revenge, Bone Breaker plunged down the ladder and dove into the bloody fray taking place on the valley floor.

For the next hour men clashed below while from the terraces of the village Kit and Mark kept up a steady barrage, picking off the reinforcements above before they could make their way down the steep cliffs that protected Stone Claw's people. The tide of the battle turned in favor of Stone Claw's warriors, and as they dispatched the last of the invaders, the Indians above withdrew to lick their wounds.

Kit's sweaty face was blackened with gunpowder when he finally strode out among the victors, who where eagerly looting the dead bodies scattered about. Kit examined one of the Diggers' arrows. In spite of the fierce battle and the blood spread all up and down the narrow valley, Kit had to grin. At least one of his nagging doubts had been answered.

The Digger's arrow was tipped in steel. It was re-assuring to know that the year was indeed still 1835.

"What do you reckon they want to talk to us about?" Mark asked as Kit steadied him. They were moving along one of the terrace walkways, with a stoic-faced warrior in the lead. Stone Claw had summoned the two of them to a meeting that had been called not long after the battle's end. Now Kit recognized the path they were taking, and in an-other minute he and Mark emerged onto the paved plaza tucked in amongst the tall towers. The post where Bone Breaker had been tied stood at one end, its severed rope still attached. At the other end, the warrior stopped at the rectangular opening in the plaza and indicated to Kit and Mark that they were to descend the ladder into the darkness below.

"I'll go first," Kit said. "That way, if you get one of them spells again, I'll be able to catch you." Kit shifted the rifle to his other hand and started down into the hole. Mark's body momentarily cut off all light from the narrow rectangle above, but as they descended into the dark pit, Kit was aware of a flickering light from a small fire below.

Kit alighted upon a dirt floor fully twenty feet in diameter, and although he had no idea what this place was, there seemed to emanate from its very walls a quiet reverence, as if this was a holy place for these people. In a circle around the perimeter of the underground hollow sat most of the warriors who had taken part in the battle earlier. As his eyes adjusted to the dim light, Kit recognized many of them, including Bone Breaker. In the center was another circle of men sitting upon odd, gray benches made of some material Kit did not immediately recognize. Stone Claw was in this circle, along with the shaman, Ghost Talker, and many of the older men, some of whom had fought valiantly only a few hours before.

Ghost Talker was chanting softly, keeping beat with a feather, and sprinkling dust into the flames of a small fire in dead center of the pit.

"Sit," Stone Claw said quietly, indicating one of the benches, where room had been made for these two expected visitors. Kit and Mark took a seat, holding their rifles between their knees.

Ghost Talker sprinkled a powder into the flames, which momentarily sparkled with a green light. Kit looked around. Overhead heavy timbers supported the roof, which in turn supported the stone slabs of the plaza above them. There was a tiny, rectangular hole in the ceiling to his left, and through it streamed a shaft of afternoon sunlight. Its rays shone overhead and struck a niche in the wall across the room, where an icon made of what appeared to be turquoise, carved wood, and corn husks stood. It reminded Kit vaguely of the carved dolls he'd seen down in Taos, in the pueblo there, but was of a much cruder design. Now, as he studied this place more closely, he noticed at least a dozen niches, each containing a small statue, but the others were mostly hidden in shadows.

The benches, Kit was startled to discover, were actually bones—bones like those in the thigh of a buffalo, only immensely larger: each at least five feet long and fatter than a man could comfortably stretch his arms around.

The air was heavy with smoke, and the mood was somber. That was understandable, Kit realized, considering the number of men of their village who had died that day. Ghost Talker prepared a pipe, took a puff, and presented the pipe toward the four directions. He next raised it up to heaven, then inclined it toward a small hole in the floor that up until now had escaped Kit's notice. That completed, Ghost Talker took another puff, then started the pipe around the inner circle of men of which Kit and Mark were members.

When it was his turn, Kit drew in a lungful of smoke, and nearly gagged. It wasn't tobacco, but whatever it was, it made his head spin and his eyes tear. He eagerly passed it to Mark and watched for his partner's reaction. If he also thought it offensive, Mark was careful not to let on. The pipe made its way back to Ghost Talker, who mumbled a little longer before setting it into a cradle near the fire.

When he finished, he gave a nod to Stone Claw and the chief began. "For many moons now, for the whole season of the snow rain and still waters, the Enemy who dwells in the land of the sleeping lodge of Father Sun has come upon my people. Many of the People have gone to the deep waters of Seguro's sleep world, and the sound of weeping has been a sad song heard in every lodge."

Stone Claw spoke to the gathered men in general, but Kit had the feeling that he was laying out the details of the past several months for his and Mark's sake. Mark's understanding of Tiwa was shakier than Kit's, but the trapper seemed to be following along without too much trouble

"Ghost Talker speaks of the ancient stories that tell of this time. That it will be the time of leaving. For more generations than any man can remember, the People have lived in this valley. I do not want to leave. I want to fight!"

A murmur of agreement began in the ranks sitting around the curving wall, swelling to a low rumble within the buried chamber.

Ghosts of Lodore

Ghost Talker raised a hand with an eagle's feather grasped in his bony fingers until the murmuring ceased. "The voices of our ancestors are strong. They grow more powerful with each passage of Father Moon. They are calling us to follow where they have gone before."

"But we do not know where this place is, this place where the ancestors have gone," one of the elders said.

"No man knows," Stone Claw agreed, "except the spirits that now dwell in Seguro's deep waters. And only Ghost Talker can speak to the spirits of our ancestors."

The features of Ghost Talker's face grew heavier beneath the weight of such a daunting responsibility. "They have not revealed this to me," he said unhappily.

"See," Stone Claw exclaimed. "It is foolish to think of leaving our home when we know not where to go. But we have already talked about this. We have come to a decision," he concluded, dismissing the topic with a wave of his hand. "For now we know what we must do."

The bottom nearly dropped out of Kit's stomach when suddenly every eye there shifted toward him and Mark. A long, uneasy silence dragged out until Stone Claw said, "All things have Father Sun, Father Moon, and Mother Earth decreed. Because of this, it is by no accident that these two strangers have been sent to us. They are mighty warriors who carry thunder in their hands."

Kit didn't like the sound of that. "Whal, fellows, the truth of the matter is, our raft broke free of its ropes and we was swept down the river. Almost drowned, we did, and I surely am pleased you men

63

happened along when you did to give us a hand. Thar warn't no deity involved. It was just a big accident, that's all." He gave them a lame grin.

They considered him in silence.

"We was just figuring on getting on our way," Kit added, hoping to disarm their scrutinizing looks.

Finally, Stone Claw spoke. "Our numbers grow smaller each time the Enemy attacks. Yet his numbers never diminish. If we permit him to return again, there will be nothing of the People left." He glanced at Ghost Talker, who affirmed the prediction with a slight nod of his hoary head. "Kit Carson, we do not ask you and your friend to fight for us. We have young warriors and the People will fight their own wars—"

That was reassuring at least.

"—but this we do ask. That you and Mark remain in the village with your thunder sticks. You are mighty warriors. You strike death to men that are far off. If you will do this, I will rally all the strong young warriors and pursue our Enemy, and take the fight to their lodges where we will defeat them. It is the only way to end this constant war."

Well, it wasn't all that much to ask, considering the hospitality the cliff dwellers had showed the trappers. All they wanted was someone to stay behind and keep an eye on the women, children, and old folks. And considering that Stone Claw was going to be taking the fight to the Diggers' doorstep, the mangy Pau-Eutaws were going to have plenty on their hands—more than enough to keep them from returning to this village any time soon.

Kit looked over at Mark, who seemed to know instinctively what he was thinking. Mark gave Kit a nod and said, "A few more days here won't make no difference one way or the other, Kit. I say we stay and lend a hand."

"I figured you'd see it that way, Mark." Kit said to Stone Claw, "We'll stay to keep an eye on the place while you an' your boys go an' do what you've got to."

Chapter Seven

They began by riding along the rocky bank of the river, but it wasn't long before the sheer walls of the canyon pinched down to the water's edge, cutting off any further progress in that direction. Both parties retraced their steps, and as Newell and Meek disappeared to the east, Bridger and Gray Feather headed west, finding the trail they had come down the day before and following it back up the steep bluffs, following a switchbacking trail suitable only for mountain goats and wildcats.

They made the high canyon rim by nightfall, built a fire, and had a quiet meal. Neither man was in high spirits, for two of their friends were lost below, and there was little hope of finding them alive. But search they must, compelled by loyalty, and by the need to know for certain the fate of their comrades. A few hours after dark, Gray Feather spotted the distant flickering of a campfire across the wide canyon on its eastern rim, and they knew that Meek and Newell had made it to the top as well.

With the sunrise, the searchers were on the move again.

Now, a few hours into the morning, Jim Bridger was stretched on his belly upon the sun-warmed rock, squinting through a brass spyglass.

"Not a sign of 'em anywhere."

Crawling carefully up alongside Bridger, Gray Feather approached the rim of the canyon as if the flat, solid rock beneath him was about to crumble away. He took the spyglass that the trapper offered to him and put it to his eye. The piece pulled the raging river in close, and in the gaps between boulders Gray Feather could just make out some of the debris washed into the canyon on the high spring run that foamed and spiraled down the narrow chutes. "It's hard to imagine anyone surviving such a harrowing course, Gabe."

Bridger frowned. "Think we're spittin' in the wind, Gray Feather. Old Kit and Mark have gone beaver this time, I reckon."

"You can't be thinking of giving up!"

"Face the facts. No man could have lived through that. And even if they did manage to survive somehow, and even if we *could* spy out two men away down thar, how in the devil would we get 'em out? Ain't two thousand feet of rope within a hunder miles of here, and if there was, we'd need a team of horses and a freighter just to haul it . . . and thar ain't no way we goin' to drive a freight wagon over them sheep trails up t' here."

In his heart, Gray Feather knew that Jim Bridger was right. But that didn't negate the fact that Kit Carson had once saved him from the Cheyenne, or that over the intervening months they had become close friends, or that he had promised to teach Kit to read . . . a pact he had yet to fulfill. "You do what you have to, Gabe, but I've got to keep looking."

Jim Bridger stood and they walked back to their horses. "Reckon I'll keep at it too, a least a little longer. You know, Gray Feather, once, a lot of years ago, I went off and left a dying man alone in the wilderness. He'd been horrible mauled by a grizzly. I figured he was about an hour or two from meeting his Maker, and Injuns were thick in the area, so me and my partner decided it was time to pull out while we still had our scalps intact. My only excuse for doing it was that I was young and scared . . . but that warn't no good excuse for leaving a friend behind. You can imagine my surprise when most of a year later the fellow shows up alive and hunting my hide for leaving him like I done. And if it warn't for the fact that he was a Christian man, I'd not be here today. He had every right to have his just revenge, and I swore later after that that I'd never do it again. So, we'll keep searching for Kit and Mark . . . at least a while longer." Peering over the seat of his saddle, Bridger narrowed an eye at the halfbreed Ute. "But there's gonna come a time when we're a-gonna have to face up to the truth."

"Maybe," Gray Feather agreed, swinging up onto his stout Indian pony. "And maybe the truth is, we find them alive."

Bridger stepped into his stirrup, giving a wince at the stab of pain from the arrowhead still imbedded in his back. "Them two's got the ha'r of the b'ar in 'em. Knowing Kit, it wouldn't surprise me none to find that him and Mark made it out with nary a scratch, and smellin' like lilac water."

"And each with a pretty gal on his arm too," Gray Feather added with a grin.

Bridger grinned too. "No, that wouldn't surprise me neither."

She looped one arm through Kit's, the other through Mark's, and together the three of them strolled along the trail that cut down the middle of the valley. They weren't alone. Although the young men had left on their mission early that morning, the village was going about business as usual. Some of the women and children worked at hoeing and planting, and maintaining the irrigation system. Others went about their daily chores of gathering food and firewood and carrying water.

Just now, Night-Sky Feather was setting off with four other young women about her own age to gather roots that grew some distance from the village down by the river. She had enlisted Kit's service under the pretext that usually a warrior accompanied them to protect them from man and beast. But both Kit and Mark saw this as a thinly veiled excuse. As they reached the mouth of the little valley, Mark drew up and gently unlatched the pretty girl from his arm.

"Reckon I ought to stay behind and keep an eye on things here. It ain't smart for both of us to be away," he said in the pidgin Tiwa language of these people, giving Kit a sly wink. Mark switched to English and added, "I get the feelin' three's gonna be a crowd, Kit. You're a lucky devil; I'd take advantage of my good fortune while I was able to, if I was you."

Kit had been raised to treat all women with deep respect, and Mark's roguish suggestion brought a bit of color to his cheeks. He was glad that Night-Sky Feather had not understood them. But then, she had made her intentions clear to him; in her

69

mind, they were destined to be married, and he was certain she'd not resist his advances. Just the same, Kit wasn't yet ready to make that sort of commitment.

"Don't you figure we've got us enough trouble without me stirring up the coals by dallying with the chief's daughter?"

Mark laughed. "Kit, you must be near blind not to see that them coals have already flamed into a full-blown fire in her heart."

"I ain't blind, Mark. I'm just ignoring it and hoping that if I don't feed it none, the spark'll go out. Because just as soon as Stone Claw gets back, we're leaving this place."

The other young women were almost out of sight on the trail ahead and Night-Sky Feather was tugging at his sleeve. Mark levered his long rifle onto his shoulder. "Well, reckon I can lead a horse to water but I can't make it drink. You do what you want, Kit. I'll see you when you get back." Mark turned and retraced his tracks to the cliff village at the head of the valley.

Kit and Night-Sky Feather caught up with the other young women and as the trail wound downward, one switchback began to pile up on top of another. The mood was somber at first because of the battle the day before, but as the village dropped out of sight the women began to chatter happily, stopping now and then to pick vibrant spring blossoms and arrange them in each other's hair. It was a pleasant morning, made even nicer each time Night-Sky Feather would skip up alongside Kit and thread a slim, bare arm through his.

"How far is this place?" he asked after they had been walking about half an hour.

"Not far," she told him. After a little while they

came to a place along the trail where she drew up
and pointed. Through a narrow gap between two
rocks Kit could see the roiling waters of the Green
River below, its anger stirred mightily this time of
the year by all the snowmelt from the high country.
He heard the roar too, and deep down inside him
stirred an uneasiness as he recalled the wild ride
the river had taken him and Mark on only a few
days before.

Soon the trail leveled off and deposited them on
a wide bench of land covered with coarse grass and
a thicket of shrubs. It was hemmed in on one side
by towering rock walls, and on the other by the
river. The river was perfectly smooth here. Kit remembered this deep, eerie section of water and its
apparent unnatural stillness—even though it was
actually flowing quite rapidly. He started down towards the river's edge, but Night-Sky Feather
caught his arm. "No, don't go near," she said, her
voice suddenly edged with warning.

Kit came back and took a seat on a rock as the
women began digging tubers from the ground near
the rocky walls. As they worked his thoughts
drifted, but always his eye was drawn back to the
glass-smooth water. The sun had climbed straight
overhead, warming the deep valley. It was a pleasant place to sit and daydream while the women
busied themselves with the chore of digging roots.
Kit let his mind wander free . . . only to find himself
staring off at the wide, flat water. Curiosity being
his bane, and probably someday his downfall, he
stood, took up his rifle, and strolled down to the
water's edge. Climbing onto a overhanging shelf of
rock, he hunkered down above the deep water and
studied it.

Here and there was that deep, queer luminosity

that he remembered from his wild ride. It was like campfires burning in the muddy-green abyss below the surface . . . dozens of them. Kit felt strangely drawn to them. Was it only his imagination? He stretched out a hand to touch the surface of the water where the nearest light appeared to be.

"Kit!"

Night-Sky Feather was standing nearby, a wide, startled look in her eyes. He grinned at her, stood, and leaped lightly off the ledge, coming to her side.

"It is time to go," she said sharply.

"What's the matter? You look like you've just seen a ghost."

"We must go," she repeated, starting away.

"Hold up thar a second, Night-Sky Feather."

She turned back, and must have recognized the questioning look he was giving her. Hugging back a small shiver, she rubbed her arms as if chilled and cast a quick glance at the river. "We are near Seguro's lair. It is not good to get too close. If he sees you, he will snatch you from the world of the living and pull you down to his sleep world where there is no escape."

Kit gave a short laugh. "Why, that's just what parents tell little children so's they don't wander too close to that thar river and fall in, is all."

But the fear in her eyes wasn't a child's fear. She fully believed the story. Kit grinned. *Injuns are the same wherever I find 'em. Even this hidden tribe has its yarns about spirits and such-like that take away the living. Whal, everybody's gotta have some sort of explanation for dying, the process being generally universal as it is.*

He didn't press her on the matter any further, and after casting one final glance at the river, which now looked unremarkable except for its calmness in the midst of the violent rapids on either end, he slung his rifle over a shoulder and accompanied the young women back to the village.

After the decision to attack the Enemy had been agreed upon, Ghost Talker slipped into a trance that lasted most of the night. When he came out of it just before dawn, he implored Father Sun, who was about to arrive, and Father Moon, who had already gone to his sleeping lodge, to spread their magic over the departing warriors. Thus reassured of their success, Stone Claw assembled his warriors and made a final inspection. Each man carried sufficient arrows, each had adorned his stone-tipped spear with a sacred hawk feather, and each wore a medicine pouch that, among other things, held small bone fragments of mighty warriors of the past who had long since gone to be with the ghosts of the ancestors in Seguro's sleep world.

As Father Sun drove the night shadows away before them, lighting their way, Stone Claw had led his small but brave band of warriors away from the village and up to the rim of the canyon. Now, several hours on the trail of the Enemy, Stone Claw stopped his men in the shade of tall rocks where a spring flowed, and permitted them to rest while he climbed to a promontory of granite and surveyed the open, desolate country that lay beyond.

A cold shiver ran up his spine. The world had opened up before his eyes, and the immense distances sent an unexplainable fear shooting through him. Only a few times had Stone Claw ventured out of the familiar confines of the valley, generally to carry on limited trade with the tribes across the mighty river to the east, or to hunt the larger game that roamed out on the plains. Never did he stay away long. There was something frightening in not having the towering rock cliffs of his home surrounding him.

Bone Breaker left the shade of the rocks and climbed up beside Stone Claw. "So much space. How do we find the Enemy out there in all of that?"

Stone Claw pulled his eyes off the fearsome openness of the territory they were about to enter. "The Enemy does not expect us to follow him. He makes no effort to hide his tracks. Following will be easy, Bone Breaker. But once we find him, that is when our task will be hard."

After a moment in thoughtful silence, Bone Breaker said, "You do not like this land. I can tell."

The older man grimaced. "It is a dangerous place, this open land where a man can see to the edges of the earth. One must move with caution. It has none of the warmth or the security that our village offers."

"Now that this Enemy has discovered us, even that security is gone."

"That is why we must overcome the Enemy this time. As our numbers grow smaller we lose the ability to defend ourselves. If we should be defeated here, then I fear all of the old prophecies which Ghost Talker speaks of will come to pass."

"There is another prophecy which you seem to have overlooked, Stone Claw."

The chief studied him, waiting. Bone Breaker went on. "The coming of men whose skin is the color of old bones, with hair on their faces and thunder sticks in their hands. We are warned to be wary of them. Is this not true?"

"You believe the strangers who we left to stand watch over our village are these men?"

"Who else can they be?"

"Ghost Talker tells us that prophecy came to pass many, many seasons ago. Can it come to fulfillment again?"

"The words of the old stories are unclear on this matter," Bone Breaker admitted. "But the stranger called Kit Carson, I sense an evil in him. I worry for the women and young ones we left behind."

"The man has truthful eyes, and his words hold no craftiness that my ears have heard. Ghost Talker discerns a warrior's spirit in him."

"He is not to be trusted with our women!"

Stone Claw's gaze narrowed upon the younger man. "Is it the *women* you are thinking about, or is it one *woman* out of all of them that you have in mind?"

Bone Breaker's face turned hard, his dark eyes flaring. "Night-Sky Feather was promised to me!"

"I detect a spirit in you which clouds true vision. You know the traditions of our people. Kit Carson kept Night-Sky Feather from the cold hands of Seguro. In that way he has won her."

"But she was promised to me!"

"I did not see that she protested the decision."

"Night-Sky Feather is only enthralled with the stranger because she has never seen anyone like him before."

"It is the custom of our people."

Bone Breaker's fist clenched the spear tighter, his knuckles blanching as he struggled to restrain the rising fury within him. "Perhaps it is the custom, but I do not accept it. Customs change. Nothing goes on forever except Father Moon, Father Sun, and Mother Earth. When this battle is over and we are back in our village, then I will deal with the pale-skin interloper!"

Bone Breaker wheeled away and marched back

to the other warriors. Stone Claw grimaced, again peering out at the frightening openness that lay before them. There was trouble ahead, and there would be trouble upon their return. The winds of change were blowing. "Nothing goes on forever," Bone Breaker had said, and now the truth of those words made Stone Claw's blood run cold.

He tried to dismiss the feeling as he roused his warriors and they once again set out on the Enemy's trail. But he knew that Bone Breaker had spoken true words. However this battle ended, Stone Claw knew one thing. Life in his village, and for the People, had somehow changed. The old ways were slowly slipping away . . . no matter how hard he wanted to deny it.

Chapter Eight

Later that afternoon Stone Claw spied the smoke of several campfires smudging the sky from behind a rise of land ahead. He brought his warriors to a halt, then led them into a declivity where they would be out of sight. Choosing three warriors to accompany him, Stone Claw set out along the declivity to determine the Enemy's strength, keeping low behind a ridge as they moved out from cover.

Using the scrubby growth of this open land, they managed to make their way undiscovered to within a few hundred feet of the Diggers' encampment. The Enemy had set up camp in the shade among some tall spires of sandstone that the desert winds had rounded and smoothed, sculpting some of the rocks into flowing arches that formed pools of cool shade in their hollows. Stone Claw counted about sixty men squatting around a dozen campfires. Mixed in with these healthy warriors were at least ten who had been wounded in the recent battle. These lay in the shade, or sat against the cool rock while others tended their wounds.

As they studied the camp, Stone Claw watched one of the warriors stealthily move out of it as if stalking something. A large lizard darted suddenly across the burning sand. At the same instant the Enemy hitched back an arm and cast a stone unerringly, stunning the creature. He pounced upon it, tore the tail off, and stuffed the reptile, live and wriggling, into his mouth. A few powerful grinds of his jaw, and the lizard was gone, and the warrior strode back to his companions wearing a wide, satisfied grin.

In another part of the camp a small company of men was systematically overturning rocks, occasionally discovering a morsel or two toward which all hands would immediately strike. One man only would be lucky, however, and the grub or insect would swiftly disappear down his throat. Then the search would continue.

Stone Claw observed the lay of the camp, their numbers, and the condition of the wounded. When he had seen enough, he and his men silently retreated and brought the news back to the waiting warriors.

"It is true that their numbers are about twice ours," Stone Claw said to the anxious party of cliff villagers that gathered around him, "but they have wounded among them, and they do not suspect an attack from us for they have not set out guards around their camp. They have stopped here, apparently, to rebuild their strength and tend their wounded. Perhaps they have sent word ahead for others to join them. If we strike at once, and without warning, we can defeat them here and now. A great success today would be a strong sign to others to avoid us."

The warriors all agreed with their chief. They wanted to strike suddenly, decisively, and then return home, for each man there felt the same apprehension as Stone Claw. These wide-open spaces were unfamiliar and frightening to men who had known only the closeness of their canyon home, and seldom ventured far from it. The warriors longed for the safety of their ancient cliff village. Wanderlust was not a quality that these people possessed in any great amount.

Stone Claw divided his men, putting an elder warrior named Bear Tooth in charge of one company while he led the other. They moved off in different directions, planning to flank the Enemy. At a signal from Stone Claw both parties were to attack at once, hoping that coming in from two sides would serve not only to confuse the Enemy, but to fool them into believing the attackers' numbers were much greater than they actually were.

Stone Claw knew that their only advantage lay in a surprise attack. The Enemy's greater numbers and more powerful weapons would mean certain defeat if the element of surprise, that great equalizer in battles such as these, was lost.

As they neared the Enemy's camp, Stone Claw deployed his warriors in a line, each man crouching behind a bush or rock as the opportunity presented itself. He drove a twig into the ground, marked its shadows with a pebble, then set a second pebble an inch to the left. His clock set, Stone Claw hunkered down, motionless, until Father Sun had made a journey equal to the time it would take for Bear Claw to move his men into position.

Slowly the shadow crept over the hot, rocky

ground. The camp remained unaware of the impending attack. Stone Claw waited patiently. Once, a big, hairy spider scurried across the ground where he lay. A sound to his left turned out to be a snake moving into the shade of a thorny copse. As it entered the bramble, a mouse scampered out. Stone Claw managed a grin, thinking that the snake had missed a fine opportunity.

The shadow had almost reached Stone Claw's pebble marker and his fist tightened around the spear in anticipation. Then a movement caught his eye. A green and black lizard racing along the hot ground with its tail held high darted past him . . . and right behind it . . .

A dark warrior wheeled to a halt, staring at Stone Claw with eyes impossibly round, and it was difficult at first to determine which man was most startled. The warrior immediately shouted a warning to his companions, but the cry died in his throat as Stone Claw's lance drove forward, impaled his larynx, and cracked through his neck bones.

But it came a moment too late. The Enemy had been alerted and were diving for their weapons. Leaping to his feet, Stone Claw cried out the signal to begin the attack. The cliff villagers raised their voices together in a hideous war whoop and charged the camp.

The first assault was repelled with a volley of arrows, and as Stone Claw watched his young warriors fall beneath them, the war chief shouted a rallying cry. Clutching up the spear of a fallen comrade, he plunged into the battle, wielding his deadly weapons with the unerring accuracy of a striking rattlesnake. In a moment the din of clashing weapons and the cries of dying men mingled in a horrible cacophony as the peaceful campsite suddenly became a stage upon which mere mortals once again were to act out an age-old drama of vengeance, with death playing the leading role.

Ghost Talker sat outside the door of his stone lodge, a bone flute at his lips, and a worn rabbit skin cape over his shoulders. The tattoo snake head upon his aged cheek stood out clear in the lowering sunlight as the shaman stared off into the west. The skull-topped stick leaned against the lodge's wall, and as the rays slanted low across the high rim of the canyon, they shot through the empty eye sockets as if the skull possessed some sort of internal illumination all its own. As Kit and Night-Sky Feather approached the old man, a low, wistful music filled the still air.

"Ghost Talker," Night-Sky Feather said softly, stopping behind the old man. The piping ceased, and as the last, sad notes wafted away towards the canyon's walls, the shaman turned, lowering the flute from his lips. The lines cut into his ancient face seemed deeper than Kit remembered, and he could see that some deep concern was weighing upon the old man.

"I have brought you your water," Night-Sky Feather said, extending the clay jug to him.

Ghost Talker acknowledged the act with a small nod of his hoary head and a faint smile that swiftly passed. "Ever since my wife went to be with the ghosts of our ancestors in Seguro's sleep world, you have seen to my simple needs, Night-Sky Feather. You are the granddaughter I never had. Your father has been like my son. You bring happiness to this old bag of bones."

"You have done so much for the People. It is a simple thing to show our respect."

Doug Hawkins

Ghost Talker accepted the pitcher and set it carefully down in front of the door to his lodge.

"For a man having just been brought 'happiness,' you're looking mighty downcast. What's troubling you, Ghost Talker?" Kit asked.

The shaman glanced at the trapper, holding him a moment in an unwavering stare. Finally he said, "You have an eye that sees clearly what is in the heart."

Kit didn't admit to the old man that what was in his heart had been plainly written upon his worried face.

"There is unrest among the spirits of our ancestors. The ghosts stir uneasily in Seguro's sleep world."

"What does it mean, Ghost Talker?" Night-Sky Feather asked, clearly worried. "Is it the warriors who have gone to fight the Enemy?"

He stared into the sky a long moment. Then, with a brief shake of his head that rattled of the bone necklace about his neck, Ghost Talker said, "I do not know its meaning . . . not yet, my child."

Kit watched the news of Ghost Talker's deep concern spread through the village faster than a coon shinnies a tree ahead of a pack of hounds. As the late shadows lengthened down the canyon, the women and older men climbed to the terrace where Ghost Talker sat in trancelike contemplation, and gathered around the shaman.

An elderly man who walked with a cane spoke first. "Ghost Talker, we must know the meaning of these things which you have spoken of to the daughter of our chief."

Night-Sky Feather stepped up alongside Kit at the back of the crowd where he was watching the proceedings over their heads. She threaded an arm through his and stood close—almost too close. Kit was keenly aware of the soft fullness of her body beneath the doeskin dress, pressing against his arm. His heart began to beat a little faster as a disconcerting but pleasant warmth spread through him. All in all, he was becoming strangely attached to this pretty Indian girl. Why, he asked himself, if she had set her sights on him, should he be so eager to dodge them?

"There is much unhappiness among the ghosts of our ancestors," Ghost Talker answered the lame man.

"Is it because of the warriors?" a young woman asked. Kit remembered watching her help one of the warriors carefully fill a quiver of those odd, featherless arrows. And later, as the men were preparing to leave, he had again seen her with this same warrior. He recalled their tender embrace, and the hesitancy to leave in the man's eyes. And when the party had finally departed, this same woman had remained watching long after they had marched out of sight.

"All I know now is what I feel . . . the restless stirring of the ghosts of our ancestors. But feelings have no substance. I cannot discern the true meaning from feelings, and if I could, I would not trust it. Feelings without substance can be most deceiving."

"What can we do to know the fate of the war party, Ghost Talker?" another man demanded.

"Yes," the first woman put in. "What can we do?"

Yet another woman spoke up. "Ghost Talker, you can speak to the spirits. They will tell you the meaning of what you feel, and of the fate of the men."

"Yes, they will tell me, if they choose to speak to me at all."

"And what is to keep them from speaking to you, shaman? They have before."

The old seer shook his head. "It is not an easy thing you ask. The ghosts must be given offerings of smoke, but it cannot come from me. It must come from a warrior."

They all seemed to understand the implication of that. All the warriors were away, pursuing the Enemy.

"Is there no other way?" the man who had spoken earlier asked.

"If I was to counsel with the ghosts concerning a child who is to be born, I would take a young mother. If to ask about the food Mother Earth gives us, any man who works the ground could make the smoke offering. But to talk of war, a warrior must offer."

"Is there no warrior left in our village?" the concerned young woman asked.

"Skull Crusher was a mighty warrior," another woman shouted, and all eyes turned toward the old man with the cane. At this Skull Crusher seemed to stand a little straighter, as if recalling past glories. Not, Kit figured, that there were many past glories to recall. From what little he had come to learn of these people, he knew that they had led a fairly peaceful life for as many generations as anyone could remember. That was why they were having so much trouble now defeating these new invaders who had discovered their hidden cliff village— these Pau-Eutaws, despised by the whites, who called them Diggers, and feared by the People, who simply called them the Enemy.

War was not in the People's nature. They were farmers, and hunters, and fishermen. . . .

Night-Sky Feather pressed herself closer to Kit

and looked up with wide, liquid eyes, like two beads of obsidian floating in a pool of milk. And they were affectionate, Kit had to admit to himself, gulping down the lump that had crawled into his throat.

"No," Ghost Talker said with a marked regret in his voice. "Skull Crusher was a brave warrior, but no more. Now he is old, like me. We have both seen more than fifty winters, and soon we will be with our friends in Seguro's sleep world. No, Skull Crusher is not the one to make a smoke offering to the ghosts of our ancestors."

At this a general state of despair descended upon the gathered people. Kit glanced over as Mark stepped up and asked what was happening.

"Thar trying to find a warrior among them who can help the medicine man talk to the spirits, to find out how the war is goin'. But it appears thar ain't any around, seeing as there all off with Stone Claw fightin' them Diggers."

"Well, the way I sees it, not knowing might be for the best, Kit, seeing as there ain't nothing none of 'em can do to help out anyway," Mark observed dryly.

"Reckon so," Kit agreed.

"I'm feelin' fit enough to be on our way jest as soon as Stone Claw gets back. But I reckon we still won't catch up with Bridger and the others till we reach the Rendezvous, what with us traveling on foot."

Kit grinned. "Won't they be in for a surprise, us two walking in like two ghosts from the dead."

They both laughed at that thought.

"Ghost Talker!" Night-Sky Feather said suddenly. "There is still one mighty warrior left in the village!" And as she spoke she started forward, her arm firmly locked around Kit's.

"What are you up to, gal?" Kit said, trying to un-hitch himself from her grip. The mumbling in the crowd died as she tugged Kit toward the old shaman.

"What in tar-nation!" Kit exclaimed, finally managing to break her hold on him. "What was that for?"

She looked at him, her wide eyes shining with pride, then turned to the shaman. "Kit Carson is a mighty warrior. He killed many of the Enemy with the thunder that speaks at his command! He can make the smoke offering to the ghost of our ancestors."

"Me?" Kit croaked.

"Yes, you," she replied.

"Yes," Ghost Talker agreed. "The spirits will accept his smoke offering."

"Me talk to the ghosts?"

They both looked at him and nodded their heads.

"Wagh!"

Chapter Nine

A procession of flickering torchlights descended the narrow trail down to the river. It was the same trail Kit had followed that morning when the women of the village had gone to collect the roots. Now the dark, dangerous way was illuminated only by a crescent moon and the torches the people carried. At the head of the party were the old men, followed by Ghost Talker and Kit, and behind them, all the rest of the villagers—except the wounded and feeble, or those mothers with very young babies, who had remained in the stone lodges to await the news that these folks would bring back. Mark Head had stayed as well, to stand guard.

At first Kit had refused the dubious honor of presenting the smoke to the ghosts of the ancestors, but that had aroused so much despair among the people that he had finally agreed. Shortly afterwards Kit had been escorted down into the ceremonial pit in the middle of the village. Ghost Talker and the elders were assembled there, seated upon the huge thigh bones around the fire. They chanted, smoked a pipe, and then, with Kit standing in their midst, each man daubed a streak of vermilion and brown paint down Kit's cheeks.

The mountain man permitted this, figuring it was something to be endured. He only wished the affair would be over with, and that Stone Claw's warriors would suddenly appear at the canyon's rim and put an end to this foolishness. Talking with ghosts, even those imagined kinds that dwell among all Indian tribes, was not a thing Kit relished doing.

But Stone Claw and his warriors never did show up, so, drawing a deep breath of resignation, and giving Mark a sideways glance and grin as they marched him away, Kit resigned himself to humoring the villagers and playing their superstitious games.

Now, on the steep trail, the procession suddenly came to a halt. Through the gap in the rocks, Kit caught a reflection of moonlight off the angry waters below. The roar of the rapids rose on the cool night air like the wail of a million disembodied spirits. Kit grinned to himself as a shiver shot through him. The villagers' superstitions were beginning to rub off, and he redoubled his effort to keep a clear head and cling to rational thought.

Some of the old men went on ahead while the people settled down upon a wide place in the trail. All this time, Ghost Talker had kept up a low chant. Now it ceased, and looking at Kit with those dark eyes that gleamed in the flickering light of the torches, he said, "You must not bring the stick that speaks thunder."

Spying a young boy there, Kit placed the rifle in

his care. "You watch after this for me, son," he said. The boy beamed as he took the heavy piece from the trapper. "Take care you don't fool with it none," he cautioned.

Ghost Talker indicated Kit's butcher knife and tomahawk as well, and reluctantly Kit divested himself of the weapons. Without them he felt naked, but he didn't expect to be running into trouble here in this isolated side canyon near the swollen Green River where no war party would be able to reach them anyway.

Resuming his low chanting, Ghost Talker led Kit the rest of the way alone. As they reached the flat, grassy place where the women had earlier collected their roots, Kit noticed that a fire was blazing down near the water's edge. The elders who had gone ahead of them to start the fire had already retreated from it and now sat motionless back against the sheer walls of the canyon. Like gargoyles of carved stone hidden in the deep shadows, they merely watched the shaman and trapper make their way alone to the fire.

"Sit," Ghost Talker said, indicating with his dog-skull staff a place by the fire.

As Kit lowered himself onto the rocky bank of the river, he looked out across the black, placid stretch of water, hemmed in on both ends by the roiling rapids. Here and there a glint of moonlight flashed off a ripple. In daylight this unnaturally calm stretch of water was uncanny enough. But at midnight, illuminated by the red and yellow flames leaping from the fire, and Ghost Talker's incessant chanting, it made the skin beneath Kit's buckskin shirt tingle as if a company of spiders were crawling up his spine.

Ghost Talker circled the fire, stretching the dog

skull over the flames, then waved the bleached bone over Kit's head a couple of times. He thrust a hand into a leather pouch and tossed a fistful of powder into the fire. It sparked green as if the powder had been transformed into a shower of emeralds. He stopped suddenly, lifted his voice piercingly to the black sky, then sat beside Kit. From one rabbit-skin bag Ghost Talker withdrew a pipe, and from another he extracted a handful of tobacco and began pressing it into the bowl.

"How long is this here ceremony gonna take, Ghost Talker?"

The shaman remained silent, as if in a trance, concentrating on loading up the pipe.

Kit grimaced. "Whal, I don't reckon it matters none. I ain't got nowhere to go t'night."

"Shhhh," the shaman said sharply.

Kit frowned and went back to watching the flames. Ghost Talker resumed his low chanting, pulling a burning twig from the fire and getting the pipe burning. Taking a few deep draws at the long stem, the shaman saluted the compass points, the black heavens above, and the shadowy ground below. "Now you must smoke the pipe," he said, passing it to Kit.

Kit could think of a lot worse ways to spend an hour or two. A pipe of tobacco looked mighty nice to him right then. He took a long pull at it and when the smoke hit his throat, he gagged and broke into a violent cough. "What is this?" he demanded, shoving the ceremonial pipe back at the old man.

"You must smoke," Ghost Talker insisted.

"It tastes like buffler patties and old rope. I can't smoke this!"

"You must smoke," he implored, "you must

smoke all of it or the spirits of the ancestors will not arise."

"Whal, then let 'em stay put!"

Ghost Talker tried to shove the pipe back into Kit's hands, but the trapper refused. A desperate concern flooded the old man's eyes. Nearly the whole village had come along on this night journey in the hope of getting some news from the spirits about the fate of the young men who had gone off to war with Stone Claw . . . and it was Kit they were depending on to get through to those spirits.

It was foolishness as far as Kit was concerned, but these folks really believed in it—believed in him. Night-Sky Feather believed in him! He recalled the gleam of pride in her dark, lovely eyes when she announced that he was a mighty warrior. And the sudden relief among these friendly cliff villagers when Ghost Talker had agreed that the spirits would come if Kit made the smoke offering.

If Kit was cursed with anything, it was with a deep-seated sense of responsibility to people who needed his help. He couldn't disappoint these folks who had helped him and Mark. Growling, he snatched the pipe back and, steeling himself against the foul smoke, took another puff.

The smoke burned all the way down his throat, but he gritted his teeth and kept puffing away. It tasted vaguely like that first pipe he'd smoked with these people, in their buried ceremonial chamber, and just as had happened then, his head began to swim and after a few moments the taste no longer mattered. Slowly he relaxed, and the roar of the cataracts on either end of the lake of still water grew distant and muffled. He was vaguely aware of Ghost Talker's low chanting. It was a pleasing sound that made Kit grin.

He looked over at the old man, and blinked with wonderment at the red and yellow bubbles emerging from the shaman's mouth. The bubbles burst, releasing the sounds of the chant as if each note had been hatched! Kit marveled at this, watching the colorful sounds drifting high up the canyon where they faded into the starry canopy. *Stars*! So that's how they come to be, he mused.

The blackness of the night was so vivid it stung his eyes. The flames seemed to pale against it, and suddenly they were way over there, as if placed at the wrong end of a spyglass! "Wagh!" Kit stared at them again, and although their heat still buffeted his face, the flames were about a mile away now!

A bit of movement caught his eye and he turned. The black surface of the river was rippling gold, green, and yellow. The colors danced across the water, swirling together, spiraling up and up and up until every bit of dancing color was in the air right above the water. Then like a golden whirlwind, it shot down the canyon and disappeared, leaving behind only the green . . . that same strange, emerald luminosity that he'd first seen on his wild ride down the cataracts. Now more than ever, the deep glow, as if from a hundred submerged campfires, held his view in an unbreakable fist.

All at once the water began to brighten as the fires beneath rose to the surface, bubbling like a witch's cauldron. The black slate surface wreathed now as the bubbles slowly ran together, growing upward from the water, taking on shapes. . . .

"Wagh! You see that, Ghost Talker?"

"They are the spirits of our ancestors."

Kit shot a glance at the old man. Ghost Talker had sprouted a pair of eagle's wings, and an eagle's beak was shaping itself from the flesh of his face.

But rather than being terrified as he rightly ought to have been, Kit was merely intrigued. He even thought the additions to the old man's features rather dashing—after a fashion.

When Kit looked back at the river, the bubbling water rose higher and higher, becoming vaguely man-shaped. In a little while—it might have been minutes, or it might have been months, Kit had lost all sense of time—the man-shaped bubbles flowed together and became men fully formed, green and yellow, slightly transparent. They floated toward the campfire, circling it and drifting close to Kit to peer intently at him with wide, unblinking eyes, as if trying to place his face—and not able to.

"Ancestors, we have called you to ask for a word on our mighty warriors who have gone away to fight the Enemy. My spirit is troubled and the People have asked me to seek the answer from those mighty warriors who have departed to Seguro's sleep world," Ghost Talker began.

"Who is this warrior that has offered the smoke?" a disembodied voice said somewhere inside Kit's clouded brain.

"He comes from the outside world. He fights bravely and commands thunder in his hands."

A floating face hovered in front of Kit, studying him, then drifted upwards to where four or five orbs of color were conferring.

"There is truth and wisdom in this one. We will tell Ghost Talker that which he seeks."

"The fate of our young men who have gone off with Stone Claw. How have they fared?"

"Many are with us in Seguro's sleep world at this moment."

All at once the black water began to glow again as if more campfires were forming within its depths, and then the faces of young men rose to the surface. A dozen or more. Through the haze, and the pulsating lights in his brain, Kit was vaguely aware of the mournful groan that had emerged from Ghost Talker's lips. And through it all, Kit was slowing growing sick to his stomach, as if he had eaten a mess of spoiled boudins.

"And what of our chief, Stone Claw?"

"Stone Claw is still among the living."

"Can you tell us the outcome of the battle?"

"The outcome is still not known. The warriors have fought bravely, but many more must yet die. The gourd of ashes is settling upon the People and they must soon go the way of the ancestors."

Ghost Talker stared into the flames of the campfire, the flickering light reflecting off his face. In a few moments he said, "But we do not know the way of the ancestors. Where do the People go from this place that has been their dwelling for all generations?"

"We will show you, now that the time has come," a voice said, and suddenly the earth dropped away, the campfire becoming but a speck as the canyon walls shot past, and then they were rising into the open sky. Kit saw the mountains all around him, and as he and the shaman rose higher, the arc of the world became apparent. Then in an instant they stopped, suspended somewhere between heaven and earth. To the south a vaguely familiar river shaped itself out of the night and glowed an iridescent green against the blackness of the world.

"There is where you must go," the voice instructed Ghost Talker. "There you will find the sons and daughters of the ancestors who have gone before you." Immediately from another part of the black planet below a vision loomed before their eyes: great cities built into cliff walls of a green mesa, others built out on the floor of a wide valley. Kit thought he recognized the shape of the mesa, as if he had once seen it from afar. In the vision thousand of peoples were streaming out of the villages, all moving toward the river. Kit watched the procession with mild surprise, then gave a small grin as if suddenly understanding what it was he was seeing—or at least what it was he *thought* he was seeing.

All at once the canyon began to rush up at them and its towering walls closed in around him again as the campfire loomed larger and larger. The plunge left Kit's stomach behind, and in spite of his smoke-numbed brain, the terror of falling gripped him, strangling him. Kit squeezed his eyes as he fought the fist encircling his throat, expecting any moment to be broken upon the rocks below. He hit the ground and a violent shudder whipped through his body. Another violent shudder gripped him, followed by another and another.

Chapter Ten

Kit opened his eyes. It was daylight and Mark was shaking him awake by the shoulders.

"Wake up, Kit! Your crying out is about to bring the whole village down on us!"

Kit groaned and drew his knees up to his stomach where he lay upon the sleeping pallet. "I'm feelin' like I'm about to heave."

"Then I better get you out of Stone Claw's lodge."

Kit pushed Mark's hands away. "Just let me lay here a while."

"All right, but if you get the urge, let me know. You must've been havin' a mighty fierce dream, what with you cryin' out that you was a-fallin' and such-like."

"It was some frightful visions, and I'll say this much, Mark. Whatever old Ghost Talker packed into the bowl of that pipe, it was powerful bad medicine. If'n these folks smoke that too much, it ain't

A SPECIAL OFFER FOR LEISURE WESTERN READERS ONLY!

Get FOUR FREE Western Novels

Travel to the Old West in all its glory and drama—without leaving your home!

Plus, you'll save between $3.00 and $6.00 every time you buy!

EXPERIENCE THE ADVENTURE AND THE DRAMA OF THE OLD WEST WITH THE GREATEST WESTERNS ON THE MARKET TODAY...FROM LEISURE BOOKS

As a home subscriber to the Leisure Western Book Club, you'll enjoy the most exciting new voices of the Old West, plus classic works by the masters in new paperback editions. Every month Leisure Books brings you the best in Western fiction, from Spur-Award-winning, quality authors. Upcoming book club releases include new-to-paperback novels by such great writers as:

Max Brand   Robert J. Conley   Gary McCarthy   Judy Alter
Frank Roderus   Douglas Savage   G. Clifton Wisler
David Robbins   Douglas Hirt

as well as long out-of-print classics by legendary authors like:

Will Henry   T. V. Olsen   Gordon D. Shirreffs

Each Leisure Western breathes life into the cowboys, the gunfighters, the homesteaders, the mountain men and the Indians who fought to survive in the vast frontier. Discover for yourself the excitement, the power and the beauty that have been enthralling readers each and every month.

SAVE BETWEEN $3.00 AND $6.00 EACH TIME YOU BUY!

Each month, the Leisure Western Book Club brings you four terrific titles from Leisure Books, America's leading publisher of Western fiction. EACH PACKAGE WILL SAVE YOU BETWEEN $3.00 AND $6.00 FROM THE BOOKSTORE PRICE! And you'll never miss a new title with our convenient home delivery service.

Here's how it works. Each package will carry a FREE 10-DAY EXAMINATION privilege. At the end of that time, if you decide to keep your books, simply pay the low invoice price of $13.44, no shipping or handling charges added. HOME DELIVERY IS ALWAYS FREE. With this price it's like getting one book free every month.

AND YOUR FIRST FOUR-BOOK SHIPMENT IS TOTALLY FREE!
IT'S A BARGAIN YOU CAN'T BEAT!

■ **LEISURE BOOKS** A Division of Dorchester Publishing Co., Inc.

GET YOUR 4 FREE BOOKS NOW—
A VALUE BETWEEN $16 AND $20

Mail the Free Book Certificate Today!

FREE BOOKS CERTIFICATE!

YES! I want to subscribe to the Leisure Western
Book Club. Please send my 4 FREE BOOKS. Then,
each month, I'll receive the four newest Leisure
Western Selections to preview FREE for 10 days.
If I decide to keep them, I will pay the Special
Members Only discounted price of just $3.36 each,
a total of $13.44. This saves me between $3 and
$6 off the bookstore price. There are no shipping,
handling or other charges. There is no minimum
number of books I must buy and I may cancel the
program at any time. In any case, the 4 FREE BOOKS
are mine to keep—at a value of between $17 and
$20! Offer valid only in the USA.

Name_____

Address_____

City_____ State_____

Zip_____ Phone_____

Biggest Savings Offer!

For those of you who would like to pay us in advance
by check or credit card—we've got an even bigger
savings in mind. Interested? Check here. ☐

If under 18, parent or guardian must sign.
Terms, prices and conditions subject to change. Subscription
subject to acceptance. Leisure Books reserves the right
to reject any order or cancel any subscription.

GET FOUR BOOKS TOTALLY *FREE*—A VALUE BETWEEN $16 AND $20

PLEASE RUSH
MY FOUR FREE
BOOKS TO ME
RIGHT AWAY!

Leisure Western Book Club
P.O. Box 6613
Edison, NJ 08818-6613

AFFIX
STAMP
HERE

no wonder they see ghosts and such-like. Ugh! You wouldn't happen to have a ladle of water handy, would you?"

Mark ducked out of the lodge, and returned a moment later with a small baked-clay bowl and helped Kit to sit up and drink. "Wonder what's goin' on out there. Folks are gatherin' from all around. What was it you seen last night?"

"Just what Ghost Talker said it would be. It was the ghosts of the ancestors, and it sure appeared the gen-u-wine article—at least at the time. Now I don't know. They was more likely ghost from the smoke, I reckon. Say, how long have I been asleep?"

"Ever since they carried you up from the river. Six, maybe seven hours now. The sun's already over the canyon wall."

"What about Ghost Talker?"

"He had a powwow with the elders. Then he went off down in that hole in the ground to be by himself."

Kit remembered the shaman's weird transformation. "How does he . . . look?"

"Look?" Mark rolled his shoulders indifferently. "He looked all right, I reckon. Kinda worried."

Kit gave out a long sigh. "Then it was all smoke after all," he said, relieved.

Mark eyed him curiously.

The light through the doorway briefly darkened as Night-Sky Feather entered the lodge. "The smoke has left your head?" she asked.

"Some of it seems to have settled down in my gut," he answered, managing a grin.

Night-Sky Feather acted as if she had not understood his feeble attempt at a joke. Her eyes were hard as black glass, and there was fear written all over her face. "The People are much worried by the vision the spirits of our ancestors have given Ghost Talker."

"I wouldn't put too much stock into them smoke visions," he said. "It was only that funny tobacco that Ghost Talker used."

She went on, not hearing his explanation. "Kit Carson, you and Mark are the only strong warriors left in the village. With your thunder sticks, you can make the warriors fight strong."

His brain was still trying to shed the poison of the smoke, and he was only now slowly catching her drift. "You're saying you want us to go and finish the fight that Stone Claw begun?"

"If you do not, Ghost Talker says many more young men will die, and the People will have to leave this place."

Mark did not understand Tiwa as well as Kit, and was a little behind, but once he had the words sorted out and strung together, he said, "We promised your father that we would stay here and watch over the village until he returns."

"Yes, but this I implore of you, or I fear that my father and the other young warriors will never return. And if the young men do not return, what will become of our village? The Enemy will return and kill all. Soon the elders will come to speak to you of this."

Kit glanced at Mark and said, "She's got a point thar. What do you think?"

"I don't know. Looks as if we might be gettin' ourselves into a passel of trouble, Kit. Them Diggers are relentless, and there are a lot more of them than there are of these folks. If'n they get it into their heads to mount a full-scale attack, you an' me might find our scalps fancying up a couple of Digger war lances."

Kit stood, taking up his rifle, powder horn, and hunting bag. He seemed to understand, even before he had consciously admitted it to himself, that he was going to end up on Stone Claw's trail sooner or later. Kit had an impulsive streak running through him Missouri River-wide and deeper than the Atlantic Ocean. More than once his father, Lindsey Carson, had warned him to listen to his head at least as often as he listened to his heart. Kit had only been a tyke back then, but he'd worked on it—he really had—and he figured in another ten or fifteen years, if he lived that long, he'd finally have it licked and become master of his rashness rather than it mastering him.

But that was looking ahead ten or fifteen years down the road, and what he knew he had to do had to be done today. Giving his partner a wry grin, Kit said, "I reckon I can't stand not knowing if them visions in my head was only from Ghost Talker's smoke, or if thar was some truth in 'em. You stay here and keep an eye on things, Mark. I'll be back as soon as I can."

Kit stooped under the low doorway out into the bright morning sunlight. From his high position on this upper terrace he could just catch a glimpse of the paved terrace below where the buried ceremonial chamber was located. Many men had gathered there, among them Ghost Talker and one of the elders who seemed to be in charge while Stone Claw was away. Kit climbed down the ladder to join them.

"Howdy," he said, and grinned at the shaman. "That was some show you put on last night. What did you pack in that pipe, anyway?"

"The spirits of the ancestors have showed you things that make our hearts heavy," the elder said.

"I know. You're fretting over the battle, thinking that maybe it's not gone too good for Stone Claw and his boys. Night-Sky Feather told me what you want me to do."

"You hold the thunder in your hand, Kit Carson. You make it do your bidding."

"Whal, I don't know about that, but this here buffler gun shoots straight as the righteous words of a parson to a wicked man's heart, if that's what you mean."

The elders gave Kit a blank look.

The mountain man grinned and said, "I come to tell you I'll go and take a look for your boys."

At the back of a box canyon, Stone Claw regrouped his battered army and counted heads. Night was coming, and with the darkness came a well-needed reprieve from the fighting. The battle had raged most of that afternoon, with the balance of power shifting one way and then the other. But slowly Stone Claw's men had given ground as the superior war-making skills of the Enemy began to tip the scales.

Stone Claw had finally retreated, leaving many dead behind, and a few wounded who had fallen into the hands of the Enemy. The small group of survivors built fires, tended their wounds, and ate what little they had with them. Afterward, with a heavy heart, the chief separated himself from the battle-weary men and stood upon a knoll of high ground where he could see the distant fires of the Enemy flickering in the blackness of the night.

The lonely call of a coyote drifted across the dark plains. Stone Claw thought of the bodies left behind, butchered now by the Enemy, and the emptiness that their passing into Seguro's sleep world would bring to the village. And he thought of the village itself. What would become of it now, drained of the vitality of so many of its young men? What was to prevent the Enemy from completely overrunning their homes when so few strong men remained to defend it?

Footsteps came softly up behind him. Stone Claw did not turn. He had already identified the visitor by his determined strides.

"Why is it the gods seem to favor our enemies? What judgment are they laying upon the People?"

Stone Claw looked at the newcomer. Bone Breaker had survived the battle with only minor wounds. He had been one of the lucky ones. Just the same, a heavy weariness had settled upon his young face. "Why do you say that the gods favor them?" Stone Claw asked. He inclined his head at the distant campfires.

"The battle turned in their favor. They have taken many of our warriors captive while we have only barely escaped to this place to lick our wounds."

Stone Claw grimaced and looked back at the far-off lights. "They have wounds to lick as well. Perhaps the battle turned, but the fight is not over."

"I have a bad feeling about what will come in the morning, Stone Claw."

The chief did not reply.

"It is clear by the worry in your face that you are worried too."

"What will come in the morning is in the hands of the gods," Stone Claw said wearily. "We have stepped across a line in the dirt, and we can never go back. We either win the battle in the morning, or we will cease to be. The village cannot fend off another attack with all her strong warriors bound in Seguro's sleep world."

"Is it not as the old ones foretold?"

"How so?"

"When the pale-skin men come the time of the People will be at an end."

Stone Claw considered, then shook his head. "I do not know the answer. The old legends tell of this, yet Ghost Talker says all that happened long ago, and that it was the ancestors who ceased to be."

The two men started back toward the small fires where the others were. "We are to stay here and fight in the morning?" Bone Breaker asked.

The chief nodded. "It is all we can do."

Bone Breaker said, "Then tonight will be our last night among the living."

"If the gods wish it, then so be it."

Before dawn, Stone Claw moved his men into position around the Enemy's camp. They kept well back to avoid the prowling sentries, and as the sun crept into the sky, a grisly scene appeared before them. Stone Claw's captured warriors had been tortured and then murdered, but what appalled Stone Claw was the ceremonial butchering that had taken place afterwards; dismembered arms, heads, feet, hands, and genitals of his young warriors, impaled upon skewers in the ground, had been put on display around a now-dead fire—one of the many the chief had seen from far off the night before.

The revolting sight had affected his men, and Stone Claw knew that if they were allowed the time to think much about it, the attack would fail. The camp was still asleep, and he judged that the Enemy had supposed his retreat to have been a permanent one. With this small advantage—and his diminished army needed every advantage it could get—Stone Claw passed the word down the line.

Each man readied his weapons, and at the chief's signal, they eased past the sentries. Then with a fearsome yell, Stone Claw stood, brandishing his weapons above his head, and attacked.

Scattered across the Enemy campsite, sleeping warriors came instantly awake, grabbing up bows and lances while the arrows from Stone Claw's battle-weary fighting men rained in. The two forces clashed, and arrows gave way to lances and knives in close-quartered fighting.

Stone Claw strove in with his war lance striking this way and that, cutting a swath through a company of men. But even as they fell, more swarmed in to take their places. Driven now by the sight of their butchered comrades, the cliff village warriors fought with superhuman zeal, for each man understood that the fate their friends had suffered would be the same fate their wives and children would suffer if they should fail here.

Bone Breaker wielded his stone war club left and right, devastating the Enemy beneath its crushing blows, and likewise, the dozen villagers that still remained standing now fought with little regard for their own safety . . . and for a brief flash of glory, they drove their foes to their knees. But the odds against Stone Claw's men were overwhelming, and slowly the tide of the battle changed.

Many of the villagers were down, some dead, others struggling as their captors overpowered them and hauled them away.

Saving them for more of your butchery, Bone Breaker thought savagely as he leaped to the aid of a nearby comrade and instantly three men fell beneath his fierce blows. Then back-to-back, these two cliff warriors stood immovable against the onslaught, their spears and clubs keeping the Enemy temporarily at bay.

At the edge of his vision, Bone Breaker saw the Enemy converging on Stone Claw. The chief was surrounded. Bone Breaker couldn't break away to aid him. All he could do was stand firm and fight for his life.

Their numbers dwindled. Bone Breaker caught a glimpse of Stone Claw being hauled away, unconscious but still alive, or the Enemy would not be taking the precaution of binding his wrists.

Realizing the fight was now hopeless, Bone Breaker sounded the call to retreat. What could he do? They had lost the battle. The only remaining hope for the People was for someone to return to the village and warn them of the next attack. If someone could at least accomplish that, then perhaps . . . just perhaps, the women, children, and old men could escape before these vicious desert dwellers could return for the final kill.

Bone Breaker broke off the fight, and leaping over the bodies sprawled across the field of battle, he and the few survivors scattered into the cover of the low-lying growth nearby.

Chapter Eleven

There was something invigorating about being out in the open, alone, striding free but with a purpose. That purpose was keeping the tracks of Stone Claw's warriors in sight. And for Kit Carson, the small signs left behind by the war party were easy to read. He preferred these open, high ridges to the closed world of the cliff villagers. He relished the soaring freedom that scanning a countryside for miles around in all directions gave him.

He'd departed the village immediately after conferring with Ghost Talker and the elders, and now several hours later, with the sun just reaching its zenith, the cliff village and high bluffs were already miles behind. If nothing else, this brisk march had flushed the last of the ill effects of Ghost Talker's smoke from his system and his head was clear, his senses sharp.

The trail he was following suddenly plunged

Doug Hawkins

down the edge of a deep ravine. The way was clogged with dense brush and years of dry weeds tumbled in by the westerly winds, but the war party's spoor remained clear to an eye schooled in such matters. Perhaps Kit could not read the marks printed on the pages of a book like his friend Gray Feather, but the marks left by man and beast in even the hardest ground were easy fodder for the mountain man's keen brain and sharp eye.

Always alert to lurking dangers, Kit now redoubled his vigilance; this overgrown cut in the land could easily hide dozens of Indians. But after a few hundred yards the fissure opened up and deposited the mountain man safely on the western slope of the range without his having encountered even a jackrabbit. Kit halted as a view of a desert basin with its wind-sharpened sandstone arches spread before his eyes. Forty or fifty miles away stood the indistinct line of yet another mountain range, beyond which Kit knew lay a vast desert and the great inland salt sea.

Kit frowned as he thought about Jim Bridger and the others. They most certainly considered him and Mark dead by this time. Most likely, the company of men were already long on their way. Kit understood that it was the only sensible thing to do.

"It's the only sensible thing to do, Gray Feather. We've looked high and low for 'em, and you know it too. That wild river went and swallowed 'em up and sent 'em on their way to Glory." As Bridger spoke, he was preparing a smoky fire of green juniper boughs. "Anyway, even if they could be found, ain't no way anyone can get down to 'em."

"There have been dozens of clefts in this canyon

106

that we could have climbed down." the Indian countered.

"Maybe, but you and me, we ain't got all summer to go scrambling up and down each and ever' one of 'em. Kit and Mark have gone beaver and it's time to face up to that."

Reluctantly, Gray Feather had to agree that was true. They had their full winter's catch of beaver plews with them, and everyone was anxious to get to the Rendezvous to trade them for powder, lead, tobacco, whiskey . . . and women. Gray Feather had at least learned that much about the trapper's way of life in the year he had ridden with Kit and these other men. It always amazed him, whenever he thought about it, that after all the grueling hardships and dangers these men went through to get the beaver, they were so willing to trade them off for a few necessities and a handful of gold—gold which generally ended up back in the pockets of the businessmen who had brought it out to the wilderness in the first place.

The economics of trapping beaver for a living somehow didn't work out—at least not to Waldo Gray Feather Smith's Harvard-educated brain. But beyond a little grumbling from these Rocky Mountain boys, most of the men accepted things as they were. A month and a half of wild abandon at the yearly Rendezvous seemed pay enough to carry them through yet another year of freezing winters, hostile Indians, and a hundred other dangers.

"A couple days more won't make any difference," Gray Feather said, "and that will still give us plenty of time to make this year's gathering at Horse Creek."

"You're right, but a couple days from now it'll be just as easy to say another couple days won't matter either. At some point you and me is gonna have to face the facts."

"All right. Two more days, and then we leave."

Bridger speared him with a quick look. Bridger was the Booshway, not Gray Feather, and it was Bridger's place to determine how many more days they would keep looking for Kit and Mark. "I'll give it one more day. That's all. *Then* I leave and you can do whatever pleases you, Gray Feather."

Jim Bridger snapped out a blanket and settled it over the smoky boughs. He held it there a moment, then pulled it away. As a puff of smoke climbed into the clear sky, he repeated the action until he'd given out his signal. From far across the gorge, the smoke was answered. Bridger rolled up the blanket and broke up the fire.

"There, I told Meek and Newell that after tomorrow we start on our way again."

The men swung back onto their horses to begin the final effort in their search for the two lost men. Gray Feather had a sinking feeling as they turned away from the rim of the canyon, for he knew as well as Bridger the slim chance they had of finding Kit and Mark now, after almost a week of searching.

At the sight of movement far down the trail, Kit crouched and scurried behind a nearby rock. As his keen eyes watched the distant figures below, he shook his powder horn near his ear, judging the shots he had left in it. The battle at the cliff village had burned much of the gunpowder he had managed to dry and salvage, and now, not knowing how long it was going to be before he reached a trading post, he had to conserve what little was left.

The approaching party disappeared around a

bend in the trail. When they reappeared they were much closer, and Kit let go of a low sigh of relief. He'd not have to burn powder just yet. He stepped out of hiding as the men came into view. They drew up short, then recognizing Kit, came forward.

Bone Breaker was in the lead. The party consisted of only five men. Nearly thirty cliff villagers had gone off to war! As they approached there was a weary doggedness to their walk.

"What happened to the others?" Kit asked, not certain he wanted to hear the answer. He recalled the haunting apparitions of the night before, and how the faces of the dead warriors arose from the deep pool of water. A part of his brain was beginning to wonder if there had been any truth to the weird visions Ghost Talker's smoke had put into his head.

Bone Breaker glared at the trapper. "What brings you here? You wish to see for yourself the bad medicine that your coming has brought upon the People?"

Kit glanced at the other four men, not recognizing any of them, then looked back at Bone Breaker. "Your people were worried. Ghost Talker had a feeling thar was trouble. They asked me to go and have a look. The others, are they dead? Stone Claw too?"

"Most have gone to Seguro's sleep world. Those who have not passed over yet will do so very soon, for the Enemy has taken them. Stone Claw is one who was taken in this morning's fight. They were many and we were few. We fought until it was made clear to my eyes that we could not have a victory. Now we hurry back to warn the others. Everyone must leave the village before the Enemy returns to make the final attack. They leave no survivors. Those they take captive they murder."

"They cut the bodies into pieces," one of the warrior added.

"How many are still back there?"

Another of the warriors spoke up. "I took a count. As near as I could see, six, maybe seven were still alive."

"How many of the Enemy are left?"

The warrior opened and closed both his fists three times.

"Thirty," Kit said. "Whal, I reckon just the six of us against that many don't stand much a chance, even with this here thunder stick." He thought it over a moment, then added, "You boys go and sound the warnin'. I'll see what I can do to spring Stone Claw and the others before them Diggers take it into thar heads to start to parcel out arms and legs."

"You? Alone?" Bone Breaker sounded incredulous.

Kit heard veiled derision in the man's words. He grinned. "I reckon I can do it alone, all right, buck. But you're welcome to tag along if'n you think I'm gonna need a hand."

Bone Breaker snapped an order to the others. "You take the warning to the village. I will go with this pale-skin warrior and see such a mighty feat with my own eyes." This time the derision wasn't veiled, but open for all to hear.

Kit levered his long rifle onto his shoulder and squinted up at the lowering sun. He'd lost his black beaver hat in the river and of all that had been washed overboard, it was the one item he missed most right at the moment. "How far you come already?"

Bone Breaker pointed at a place in the sky where

the sun had stood about three hours earlier.

"We best be making tracks then if we intend to pull Stone Claw and the others from the fire before night comes and them Diggers decide to make mincemeat of 'em," Kit said. Without waiting for Bone Breaker's reply, the mountain man resumed his march.

The Indian fell in step with Kit, his war lance swinging at his side and his sullen, brooding face staring straight ahead. They continued on this way for most of an hour, and although Kit was never much for small talk, he figured that a cigar-store Indian would have gabbed his ear off by comparison. This dead silence was beginning to gnaw at him. He knew what was eating at Bone Breaker, but wasn't sure how to broach the subject. Over the last few days he had grown comfortable with Night-Sky Feather, and the idea of having her at his side and sharing his blanket had become downright attractive.

"Whal, it ain't as if I went outa my way to win her over," Kit said all at once, breaking the deadly silence. "It was your customs that moved the gal in my camp in the first place. All I done was save her life."

They walked on in leaden silence another fifty rods.

"Since the day you came to our village, only bad medicine has fallen upon my people."

"Wagh! Whal, now that's a fine how-de-do! I reckon Mark and me showin' up is what caused them Diggers to find your hidden valley? Heh? Between him an' me we kilt nearly a dozen of 'em for you."

"We could have fought them off," Bone Breaker countered. "Just as we have done for six passages

111

of Father Moon. It was because of you that Stone Claw decided to follow the Enemy out of our safe village and attack them in their own camp."

Kit laughed. "I seen all them empty lodges. Sure as river water wears out stone, the Enemy was slowly killing off your people. Stone Claw did the only sensible thing he could . . . he went after the varmints. You can't let bad men go unpunished or before long the countryside will be overrun with 'em."

Another long silence descended on them, chaffing the trapper like an overtight collar. Kit was getting mighty impatient with this Indian, and he could see that Bone Breaker was seething with anger toward him. Well, Kit didn't altogether hold it against the man. He obviously cared deeply for the girl. Just the same, Kit didn't know what he ought to do about it—or even *if* he ought to do anything about it.

"You cast some kind of spell over Night-Sky Feather, or she would not have fallen from the terrace. You knew the customs, that is why you did it. The visions of the ancient ones speak of men with pale skin and hair on face. Men who carry thunder in their hands and have breasts that shine like sunlight. They tell us to be wary of such."

"Shiny breasts? Bull feathers! You've got your history all stirred up the wrong way, Bone Breaker. Them was the Spanish conquistadors you just described, and they come through here a few hunder years back or so. Them aren't no special visions. Thar stories of what already happened, passed down through the generations."

"You mock the old ones?"

Kit drew to a halt and narrowed an eye at the scowling warrior. "You listen to me, buck. I don't

mock no one on account of what he believes. If you
want to make your history into your religion, whal,
that's just fine and dandy with me. But right now,
we got us about thirty Diggers what intend to make
hash meat outa your partners. Now, I'm figuring to
shove a stick through thar spokes if I can, and I'd
be obliged to you for your help. But if all you want
to do is stir up a poison pot between us, then you
best turn around right here and go back to your
village with the others."

"Night-Sky Feather was promised to me!" Bone
Breaker shot back.

"So it comes back to that."

"She was mine!"

"Yep, she *was*. But she ain't no more. Get used to
it."

Bone Breaker lunged for Kit's throat. The mountain man saw it coming and sidestepped, swinging
the barrel of his rifle against the side of the warrior's head. He went down, stunned, shook the fog
from his brain, and launched himself again at Kit.

The two men tumbled to the ground, fists flying,
scrapping and gouging like two wild animals. Bone
Breaker was a hard, wiry man, but Kit had been
well schooled in frontier fighting, having cut his
teeth on battling hostile Indians, drunk Mexicans,
emotional Frenchmen, and hot-tempered Irish-
men. In every case it was the one who kept a clear
head who came out on top.

Bone Breaker hadn't even thought about the flint
knife in his sheath. They were fighting over a
woman, after all, and that generally brought out the
most primal instincts. Man-made weapons be
damned! Kit figured the enraged warrior just plain
wanted to shred him with his God-given weapons.

Across the ground they rolled, Kit managing to

113

keep the other's claws and teeth just out of reach
He saw an opening and swung an elbow into the
man's jaw. It had little effect. Kit followed with a
low jab to Bone Breaker's belly, momentarily
knocking the wind from his opponent. In that in
stant, Kit broke Bone Breaker's grip and sprang to
his feet, crouching as the other regained his footing
and lunged again. Kit sidestepped, shooting a left
jab that smacked solidly against flesh and bone.

The warrior staggered back, clutching his jaw
Kit saw his chance and threw two low punches
doubling the fellow over, then standing him
straight up on his toes again with a powerful up
percut. Kit's peculiar mixture of fisticuffs and Ren-
dezvous-style donnybrooking was confusing at
best, disastrous at worst to this warrior who had
known little more than the tactics of the cliff village
people.

Kit feigned to the left, moved right, then without
warning dropped low and swung out a leg, knocking the pins out from under Bone Breaker. The man
crashed hard onto the trail and lay there stunned
as Kit dove onto him and in a flash grabbed a hank
of hair and drew his butcher knife, pressing it
against the warrior's scalp.

"I'd lift your hair here and now, buck, but if I did
you wouldn't be much help in freeing Stone Claw
and the others, now would you?" Kit was breathing
hard.

Bone Breaker's suddenly wide eyes were rolled
up in their sockets as if straining to peer through
his skull at the keen knife blade lightly touching his
skin. "What is this you do?"

"We call it scalping, and if you happen to survive
it you'll carry around the meanest-looking scar you
ever did see. It will be something to tell your chil-

dren about . . . that is if you can find some squaw to marry you afterward so's you can *have* children."

Bone Breaker gulped and Kit grinned.

"No, reckon you wouldn't know about scalping. Them stone knives you use ain't hardly up to the job of properly removing a man's topknot all in one piece. You want to continue this or smoke the peace pipe?"

Although at first stunned by Kit's victory over him, Bone Breaker had regained some of his earlier bravado. "I'll make the peace . . . for now. But after we have finished what we must do, then we finish this."

Kit laughed. "You ain't in much of a position to bargain. I can finish you off here and now and go after Stone Claw by myself like I started out to do." He released his hold on the young warrior. "But I'd rather have your help, if you're still willing to give it."

Standing, Kit backed away from the warrior . . . right into the point of a war lance. In an instant a half-dozen Diggers leaped from the cover of nearby rocks and surrounded them.

Chapter Twelve

"They must have trailed you and the others after
you escaped," Kit surmised as he and Bone Breaker
marched side by side, their hands securely tied behind them with leather thongs. The Diggers had immediately taken them captive and relieved them of
their weapons and all their possessions—everything that could be easily removed. The medicine
bag that Bone Breaker wore around his neck, they
left, as well as the spare bullet pouch that dangled
at Kit's belt—a stroke of good fortune that brought
a tight grin to Kit's face.

His rifle, tomahawk, butcher knife, powder horn,
and hunting bag, as well as Bone Breaker's war
lance, club, and flint knife, had all been divvied up
between the small band, with the leader claiming
the best prize for himself. Kit's buffalo rifle.

"The old stories spoke truly," Bone Breaker said.
"The pale-skin men bring only trouble."

"I'm gettin' mighty tired of hearing about the 'old stories,' buck. Time to get your head outta the past and help me figure out how we're going to break free of this here pickle barrel before these Diggers decide to start cutting on us."

The muzzle of Kit's rifle barrel smacked into his spine. He winced, and when he turned, the scowling warrior in possession of it said, "No talk."

The mountain man shifted his eyes back to the trail ahead, and the bleak landscape with its weirdly wind-shaped rocks scattered here and there across the miles of thinly vegetated sand. They walked on for mile after mile with the afternoon sun hot upon their shoulders. Although it was still only spring, this basin had heated up like an oven, with little shade anywhere to offer.

The Diggers chattered among themselves, and from what Kit was able to pick up out of their conversations, he learned that there was a big victory dance going to be held that night, and that he and Bone Breaker, and the others who had been taken that morning, were going to be the featured entertainment for the evening's ceremony.

But Kit still had an ace up his sleeve. If only he could figure out how he was going to play it . . .

After about an hour the Indians brought their prisoners to a small stream and let them drink. Then setting them near a rock that afforded at least a smattering of shade, the Diggers spent some time by the water, drinking deeply and splashing the sweat and dust from their faces.

Kit knew that if these warriors succeeded in bringing him and Bone Breaker into the larger war party at the Diggers campsite, their hope for escape would fade all together. If they were going to make an attempt, now was the moment.

They had been placed in plain sight of the war party, although no guard was posted over them. After all, they weren't going anywhere, tied up as they were.

"Bone Breaker," Kit said softly. The warrior inclined his head closer. "Think you can reach the pouch on my belt?"

Bone Breaker glanced over and said, "Turn a little and I can."

Kit waited until all eyes had turned away, then carefully scooted closer.

"I can reach it now," the Indian said, stretching his bound wrists back.

"Open it up. Thar's a little knife in it," he said, calling his shaving blade a knife since there was no word in Tiwa for "straight razor."

Both men froze when a Digger strode up from the stream, slinging the cool water from his dark face. It was the leader who had appropriated Kit's rifle. He peered down at the two prisoners and checked the straps that bound their wrists. Satisfied that they were still tight, he walked back to his partners.

"Quick!" Kit whispered. "We ain't got but a few moments before they get us moving again." They inched closer together, and Bone Breaker reached back and fumbled with the pouch, working it open with his fingers. Awkwardly, he managed to extract the razor.

"This is a knife?"

"Just hold it so's I can get a grip on the blade. It's all folded into the handle."

This was something that clearly confounded Bone Breaker, but Kit hadn't the time to explain the matter to him. In an instant Kit had levered the blade from its bone handle, and taking it from the warrior, began to saw away at the leather thongs that bound the other man's wrists.

The straps fell away and suddenly Bone Breaker was free! Kit saw in a moment of hesitation that the cliff warrior was entertaining some thoughts on this turn of events. He could easily flee and make good his escape from these warriors if he chose to do so now. That would be a simple solution to the problem of this outsider who had come between him and his woman. . . .

But in the next instant he grabbed the razor, and in a second Kit's wrists were free as well. That had answered one of Kit's questions. When the chips were down, he could count on Bone Breaker's loyalty—in spite of their personal differences.

"Soon as no one's looking let's skedaddle around that thar rock." Their opportunity came when one of the Diggers splashed another. Laughing, all the other warriors broke into some horseplay and dunked the perpetrator.

Kit and Bone Breaker darted off in different directions, and regrouped behind the rock. All Kit had was the razor, a meager weapon at best. Bone Breaker grabbed a fist-size rock and after hefting it two or three times to judge its weight, appeared quite content with his chosen weapon.

"Let's spread out some," Kit whispered. Even as the two men crept off to position themselves, a shout of alarm rang from the Diggers and, grabbing up their weapons, they scrambled off in all directions. Kit put Bone Breaker out of his mind. They were each on their own now, and they'd each have to make the best of it.

Kit hunkered down out of sight until the first warrior came near. Rushing up behind him, Kit grabbed a handful of hair and yanked back to bare the man's throat. One quick slice and down he went with his life force spurting violently through clenching fingers. Kit snatched the tomahawk from the man's breechclout, and instantly threw himself aside as a war lance whistled through the air and thunked into the sand.

Rolling into a crouch, Kit heaved back and let the tomahawk fly. As the short ax rolled through the air toward its target, the trapper yanked the war lance out of the ground, wheeled, and thrust it deep into the belly of a third attacker who was rushing up behind him.

Wrenching it free, he wheeled again and swiftly took in the scene that lay before him. Three dead and no more attackers coming at him. There was some scuffling coming from behind the rock. Leaping across the open ground, he arrived in time to watch Bone Breaker crush the skull of one of two men there. The other had already joined the ghosts of his ancestors. Kit took a quick count. Five. There had been six!

"Where's the other one?" he snapped.

Bone Breaker lowered the bloody rock and pointed at the man fleeing down the trail.

"Can't let him get away and sound an alarm!" Kit glanced around and spied what he was looking for. Snatching up the rifle, the mountain man drew back the hammer, checked that the cap was still in place, and settled the long wooden fore end atop a rock. He steadied the sights and squeezed the trigger. The rifle boomed and two hundred yards down the trail the last Digger lunged forward and burrowed headfirst into the ground.

Kit lowered the rifle and slowly stood, taking in a deep, calming breath. It was all over and he had

managed to best the odds again. He wondered
briefly, as he collected his gear from the dead men,
just how long his luck would hold out. Sooner or
later . . . but no, he refused to think about that just
now.

Bone Breaker's eyes lingered on the rifle a moment. "That is not the sound of thunder," he said
after a considering what he had seen and heard.

"You're right. It ain't."

"It is a thing made by men."

Kit laughed. "Welcome to the nineteenth century,
Bone Breaker." He glanced at the low angle of the
sun. "We better make a fast march if we're going to
get to that Digger camp before nightfall."

They collected all the arrows the Diggers had carried, two bows, and a couple of war lances, and set
off on their journey.

"There are even more of them than I remembered," Bone Breaker said softly. "They must be
coming in from other camps."

"That's encouraging," Kit replied dourly. "Do you
see the prisoners?"

Bone Breaker studied the crowded campsite.
"Over there." He pointed past the clump of bushes
behind which they had crept. The camp below
them was a haphazard affair scattered out over a
couple of acres of rocky ground. Kit's gaze followed
the young warrior's finger to where Stone Claw and
five others were bound hand and foot.

"Least we know thar still breathing."

"For now," Bone Breaker added dubiously. He
glanced over, a taunting curl coming to his lips.
"How *are* you going to free them? I came all his way
with you to see this mighty feat."

Kit had no idea *how* he would do it . . . yet. But he wasn't about to give this gloating Indian the satisfaction of telling him so. He ignored the sarcasm in Bone Breaker's voice, returning a confident grin instead.

"Whal, the first thing I'm going to do, buck, is wait till it's full night." *And hopefully by then I'll have thought of something,* he added to himself, staring up at the darkening sky. If he ever *was* going to think of something, he'd have to do so pretty fast.

In the waning daylight Kit tallied up the warriors. There were more than a dozen wounded men among the healthy, but not counting them, Kit figured that he and Bone Breaker had a little over forty armed men to deal with. He'd never studied at West Point, but it didn't take military training to figure out that the odds were stacked against them.

Well, he had already known that before starting out. What he hadn't known, and what he was studying now, was the lay of the camp and of the land around it. A shallow gully cutting around back of the camp caught his eye. It would gather shadows faster than the open land, and hold them closer under the faint light of the moon and stars. Using it, a stealthy man could work his way to within a few dozen feet of where Stone Claw and the others were fettered and guarded. Kit glanced at the Digger bow in his hand and then at the quiver of arrows at his elbow. A germ of a plan was taking root as his view shifted purposefully toward Bone Breaker.

"What is that look for? I don't like what I see in those pale eyes."

"You know what, Bone Breaker? I just thought of something."

"I am almost fearful to ask what."

"In the dark, one Injun looks pretty much like any other Injun."

"I had the same thoughts about you the first time I saw you and Mark."

Kit grinned. "Now listen up. This is what you and me is a-goin' to do."

As night's blackness crept across the desert floor, the Diggers built a big fire and began whooping and dancing to the rattly music of clacking sticks and a rhythmic pounding that sounded to Kit like someone hammering on a hollow log. He didn't pay attention to the music, but the big fire in the center of camp at first concerned him. After they had fed it every dry piece of wood within a hundred miles, however, Kit's worrying stopped. The flames leaped so brightly that any Digger glancing away from them into the night would be totally blind for at least five minutes.

With his hopes for success bolstered, Kit motioned for Bone Breaker to move into position. The warrior gathered up the bow, quivers, and war lance. Kit checked his rifle and slung a bow and quiver of arrows onto his back. Easing out of cover on his belly, he began the long crawl through the gully.

By the sound of it, this Indian fandango was just getting started. Kit hoped it would build for an hour or two before Stone Claw and the others were hauled over to provide the evening's main entertainment. He moved slowly, carefully, stopping every few feet to observe the carryings-on and make certain he had not been spotted. But there was little likelihood of that since most of the warriors were gathered around the bonfire in the center of the camp, leaving only a few scattered guards to keep an eye on the prisoners. And these were watching the dancing around the fire as well, which practically guaranteed Kit wouldn't be seen.

Well, why should they be overly cautious now? They had routed the cliff villagers, hadn't they? No one would expect the few vanquished survivors to return, especially since the Diggers had sent out a war party to finish them off.

Kit, for his part, avoided looking at the bright flames, preserving his night vision for the task at hand. Ten minutes of slow going brought Kit directly behind the guards and their prisoners. In the reflected light, the trapper noted that several of the cliff villagers were in a bad way. Stone Claw had a dark splotch on his face that Kit suspected to be dried blood. In fact, every one of them appeared in some way wounded. Kit's high hopes drifted southward as he tried to imagine how he was going to haul a bunch of wounded men out from beneath the enemies' noses where even hale and hardy warriors would have difficulty escaping.

Two guards lounged nearby, each gnawing on something that looked like a fat cigar made of dried leather. But knowing the peculiar diet of these Indians who seemed always on the verge of starving, Kit figured it might be anything from a hind leg of a dog to the dried remains of a rattlesnake, and he preferred not to speculate on the matter any further. He silently removed the quiver and bow, and set aside a war lance that he had carried in the same hand as the rifle. Both guards were watching the dancing in the middle of the camp now, and there was a chance he could come up behind one of them without being seen by the other.

The drumming and stick rattling became louder,

and the whooping and dancing more energetic, almost as if the activities were reaching some sort of high point. It brought to mind the fandangos he'd been to in Taos, when a gent would throw down a wide-brimmed hat in the middle of the dance floor and all the couples would step back to give him room. The music always picked up then just the way it did now, and that fellow—if he was good—would high-step and fancy-foot his way around the brim of that hat faster and faster until a man's eyes went crosswise just trying to follow along.

Kit grinned. And it was always about that same time that some of the señors who had drunk too much *aguardiente* would get their hackles up because the mountain men in attendance always seemed to woo the prettiest señoritas away from them. Then they'd have a grand free-for-all, with the mountain men forting up back-to-back in the center of the dance floor to take on all comers. But they always managed to skedaddle out of there one step ahead of the *alcalde*'s police.

Kit shook his head wistfully. He sure did miss Taos. But he had to get his mind back on business. He knew that by now Bone Breaker was preparing to make his entrance and, with any luck, his appearance would distract the enemy even more. Drawing his butcher knife, Kit elbowed his way out of the gully and, at a snail's pace, made his deadly way toward the nearest guard, praying that the bright firelight and energetic party-making would cover his approach. . . .

Suddenly the music stopped and everything came to an instant standstill. Kit flattened himself and held his breath. He was out in the open with no cover other than what the darkness afforded. A few feet in front of his nose the guards stirred and began hauling the prisoners to their feet.

With hope fading, Kit understood what had happened. He had arrived too late. The slaughter was about to begin.

Chapter Thirteen

Four of the fierce Enemy fell in place alongside Stone Claw and his beleaguered men. Stumbling under the prodding points of the Diggers' war lances, the prisoners approached the fire. They were strung out in a line, faces toward the flames, backs in shadows. Slowly a low chant began, growing as more voices and the clacking of sticks joined in. One of the Diggers drew a knife from the waist of his breechclout and stalked back and forth between the prisoners and the fire.

It was plain that he was choosing his first victim, and it was just as obvious that he was drawing out the process to arouse as much dread in the bound men as he could. Drawing out the agony was apparently part of the ceremony.

Kit glanced to his left and spied a bundle of sticks that had been held in reserve to kindle a new fire. Slithering over, he flattened behind the pile of tinder and quickly removed his steel and flint. Sprinkling a little gunpowder on a piece of waxed cloth that he carried along to help build fires, Kit struck a spark, and then urged the glowing specks into a small flame with a puff of his breath. Kit's view jumped from the tiny fire he was trying to start to the roaring blaze in the center of the camp.

"Burn," he whispered, "burn!"

The man with the knife continued to stalk, eyeing the cliff villagers as a fox might a row of plump chickens asleep on their roost. From time to time he'd leap toward one of them. The intended victim would cringe back, but at the last moment the executioner would stop, his knife hovering only inches from the intended victim's breast. Then the camp would laugh and the process would begin all over again.

Kit's little fire had caught some of the twigs and now was eating its way up through the thicker branches.

The executioner now changed his tactics and moved behind Stone Claw's warriors. With knife held high, he slowly made his way along the line, pausing at each man's back, then moving on. No one knew when the first fatal blow would come . . . and that was the whole point of this routine, Kit figured.

The executioner came back down the line, and this time he halted behind Stone Claw. The pause this time was longer, and as Kit watched, the knife lifted a fraction higher. Kit scooted away from the crackling tinder and, putting elbows to the ground, he hefted his long rifle to his shoulder.

Just then every head turned.

Right on cue, Bone Breaker strode boldly into the camp as if it was home to him—except that he had an arrow already nocked into the bow. To the Diggers who had just glanced from the bright flames, he must have looked like one of their own—one of the men sent on to trail the escaping cliff villagers. But coming in alone like this could only mean one thing to these desert warriors. The others must have been killed.

The ceremony came momentarily to a halt as one of the Diggers strode across to meet this new arrival. At that same moment someone spied the fire that Kit had started. With a shout of alarm a company of men jumped to beat it out with their blankets.

It was only then, when the first man was within ten feet of Bone Breaker, that the Digger discovered the ruse. With a startled shout of warning to the others he lunged for Bone Breaker, and the cliff warrior drew back and sent an arrow through his heart in reply.

By the bonfire, the executioner suddenly comprehended what was happening, and without hesitating he lifted the knife above Stone Claw's shoulder blades for the killing blow. But before he could strike, an explosion at the edge of camp startled them all. The executioner's skull burst like a ripe pumpkin and the camp was in instant confusion.

Confusion of this sort only lasts a few seconds before men regroup. Kit understood this well, and in those fleeting moments he leaped to his feet and dashed across the camp, plowing his way through confused men diving for their weapons.

He wielded the heavy barrel of his rifle like a scythe, harvesting Diggers right and left. He halted once and rammed the rifle butt back and low into the midsection of a Digger coming up behind him;

then, whirling around with his tomahawk, he slashed through the man's throat. A step to one side took him out of the path of a war lance that missed by a cat's whisker. Kit retaliated instinctively and smashed the nose of his nearest attacker with another jab of the rifle's curved steel butt plate. Then he was at Stone Claw's side. The chief was as confused as the others, but when the leather thongs that bound his wrists fell away and Kit thrust a war lance into the man's hands, he knew instantly what to do.

Stone Claw kept the Diggers at bay while Kit sliced the rest of the cliff villagers free. Passing out the bow and arrows, his butcher knife and tomahawk, Kit shouted, "Into the night, men!"

He glanced past the fire to Bone Breaker, who was fending off almost a half-dozen men, pressing in closer and closer around the cliff warrior.

"Get your men outa here, Stone Claw," Kit shouted above the din of the battle. "We'll meet up later."

He dashed through the melee, ducking arrows and dodging the stabbing thrusts of war lances. His empty long rifle was little better than a war club now. But it had both reach and weight, and wielding it overhead, Kit had stepped out of the present, leaving modern nineteenth-century technology behind and reverting to the primeval hand-and-club warfare that had served man for thousands of years. The violent juices of the battle were coursing through his veins as he joined the fighting at Bone Breaker's side.

"I got the others free. Now it's time for you and me to cut and run," Kit managed to say between parrying spear thrusts and cracking skulls.

Bone Breaker's stone battle ax snicked this way

and that with lightning speed, crunching bone with unerring accuracy. The two men battled back-to-back, barely managing to keep the pressing enemy at bay.

"I am ready," the Indian answered, breathing hard. In the leaping firelight sweat glistened orange and red off his dark skin and mingled with the streams of blood that ran from half a dozen small wounds.

"Let's skedaddle before we both go beaver!" Kit drove the barrel of his rifle between the eyes of the warrior in front of him, then snapping the rifle butt forward and up, he punched a hole in the attackers' ranks. Whirling the rifle overhead, he and the cliff warrior dove through the gap and raced into the night like a pair of deer two steps ahead of a hungry grizzly bear.

"We are all here but Morning Singer," Stone Claw said after a head count was taken. The small company of escapees had managed to find each other and regroup in a dark declivity a mile or so away. "Morning Singer fell beneath their arrows, and I could not save him."

From their hiding place, Kit could see the prick of light that was the bonfire far off in the night. They were too far to hear the angry ravings of the Diggers that he knew must be ringing through the camp right now. That they had escaped at all was nothing short of a miracle, with a large helping of good luck thrown in.

"Whal, I say we done the best we could," Kit replied, running a ball down his rifle barrel and thumbing a cap onto the nipple. He carefully lowered the hammer and with the piece loaded and primed, he felt like he'd stepped back into the present. He ran a hand along the battered and scarred wood, discovering a few new gouges where the fore end came nearly flush with the muzzle. He also found a hairline crack on the rifle's wrist just behind the lock plate. That would have to be repaired soon or Kit risked losing the use of the firearm.

"Thar getting together a party right now to come after us, if I ain't missed my guess. If we hurry we can make it back to your village before sunrise and dig in before they make thar attack."

Wearily the men stood and began the long trek. Kit told Stone Claw that he'd catch up with them.

"Where are you going?" Bone Breaker asked.

"I'll keep an eye on your back trail for a piece. When I see them coming I'll catch up. Your wounded ain't going to be able to travel much faster than a lame dog, so I'll have to figure out a way to topple a tree or two in thar path."

There weren't any trees around, of course, and Bone Breaker merely looked confused at Kit's reply. Then he dismissed this pale-face stranger's odd comment and lent a hand to one of the men who had a bad leg wound. As the ragtag party of survivors started back to the village, Kit turned back and, falling into an easy dogtrot, retraced the steps of their hasty retreat.

At a place that overlooked the campsite, he elbowed into position. Below, the camp was busily organizing itself; wounded over here, dead over there, and near the bonfire the remaining healthy warriors who were not needed to tend the bleeding were stringing their bows and filling their quivers. It was just as Kit had suspected. They were planning a retaliatory raid on the cliff villagers—and this time they would not retreat. There were so few fighting men left among Stone Claw's people that retreat would not be necessary.

He waited until the war party was about to depart. Then slipping silently back, Kit fell into his easy, mile-eating lope. He moved up the trail with the surefootedness of a mountain goat, his eyes fully adjusted to the dim starlight that showed the way. After a while he stopped and moved off the trail. The Diggers were far behind him, but eventually their shadowy forms became just barely visible down the trail. Once again Kit fell into his easy trot, wondering how far ahead Stone Claw's battered party was.

After another couple of miles he again drew off the trail and lingered in the shadows, and thus for the next couple hours he kept tabs on the Diggers' progress. But this couldn't last forever, and eventually Kit overtook the homebound warriors. They had just started into the brush-clogged ravine that Kit recalled descending earlier that day when he trotted up behind them.

"Thar only a couple miles back, Stone Claw."

In the deep shadows Kit saw the heaviness settle in the chief's face. "We cannot fight them here and now. Our weapons are few, and the men are already asleep on their feet."

"Someone needs to fly ahead and warn the village," Bone Breaker urged.

Kit agreed, but added, "Let's hope that by this time the other returning warriors have already spread the warning, and your people are already leaving."

Stone Claw said, "There are many old men and women. How far could they flee? And even so, the Enemy would pursue them without ceasing, like a dog that roots at a burrow where the scent of a rabbit is strong."

Kit grimaced. What the chief said made sense. "Whal, looks like the time has come to make a stand, Stone Claw. Your village is a right hard place to get at. I reckon it would be the best place to fort up."

"But only if the Enemy can be stopped long enough so that we might return and make the preparations."

"You're the chief and you got to do as you see fit. But if it was me, I'd send my fastest runner ahead to tell the women and old men to start making up arrows and gathering together as many war lances as they can lay hands on. That's the only move you have left as far as I can see."

Stone Claw nodded. "It is as you say. There is a time when men must stand and fight, and may the outcome be in the hands of Father Sun and Father Moon." Stone Claw grew silent, his dark eyes peering down the path they had been following. Kit understood what the chief was thinking.

"You just get your boys moving on home, Stone Claw. I'll figure out a way to hold them Diggers here long enough to give you the time you need."

The chief said, "If you can do that, Kit Carson, then we will be ready for the Enemy when they come." Turning to Bone Breaker, he said, "You are the fleetest of foot. Fly ahead to the village as you already have said. Bring the word of the chief to our people. Weapons are to be gathered and arrows made; then water must be carried into the lodges where all the little children and women are to seek refuge. Let the old warriors keep guard at the doorways and drive the Enemy from the lodges while we who remain fight them on the cliffs of our home."

Bone Breaker turned up the declivity and disappeared through the thicket. When he had gone, Kit said, "You and your boys best get a move on now too. Them Diggers ain't far behind. I'll catch up."

The chief ordered his men back on the trail and followed Bone Breaker. Once again Kit was alone, and all he had to do was keep twenty or thirty warriors occupied for a couple of hours while Stone Claw's band hurried home, he thought wryly.

But he already had that part figured out. A thin grin creased Kit's face as he fished out his flint and steel, and for the second time that evening commenced to kindle a fire.

At least now Mother Nature was working for him instead of against, as it so often might seem to a man who lived summer and winter in the wilderness. Tonight she had provided a steady westerly breeze blowing strong from the valley floor into this narrow ravine. And since there was a well-worn trail through it, Kit suspected it was the only convenient doorway to the mountains directly behind him for miles around.

He built his fire behind a rock where its light would not be easily seen. Stepping out around the rock, away from the light of the flames, he could see far down the trail. When he spied the first of the marching shadows far off, he quickly spread the flame to the tightly packed piles of dried weeds that the wind had blown in over the years. Soon the quiet night air was filled with the growing crackle of burning twigs as the flames ate their way into the weeds. The land brightened blindingly all

135

around him and a dense, choking smoke settled heavily in the ravine.

Kit hurried up the trail, halting halfway to the top to look back. The mouth of the ravine was already a roaring inferno that no man could possibly enter and live. This fire would burn its way up the ravine for hours. It would be at least morning before Diggers could follow Stone Claw's lame band of warriors.

Up on top, Kit looked back one last time. The flames below were leaping and shooting dozens of feet into the air. Beyond them the Diggers' pursuit ground to a halt as infuriated warriors crowded together on the trail, pointing and stomping in frustration. All they could do now was wait. Grimly considering the few extra hours' reprieve that the fire had given the villagers, Kit knew it would not be nearly enough

He hurried on his way, and soon caught up with Stone Claw. Behind him the night sky shimmered with the glare of the dancing flames, a display equal to any of the Northern Lights Kit had observed.

"That should hold them until morning," Kit said.

"Then when Father Sun returns to the sky, we will be ready for them," Stone Claw replied stoically, but just the same Kit caught the guarded note of despair that slipped past the chief's words.

Kit lent a hand with some of the wounded, and for the rest of the night they wound their way back into the mountains, toward Stone Claw's hidden valley above the Green River.

Chapter Fourteen

The whole village was writhing in anguish, waiting for Stone Claw and the others to return. The earlier group had brought the shattering news of the warriors' defeat, the captivity of the few remaining survivors—and Kit Carson and Bone Breaker's return to attempt a rescue.

Then several hours later Bone Breaker had showed up with word of the impending attack and Stone Claw's command to start gathering weapons and putting up water and supplies in the lodges for the women and children.

The hours of waiting were almost as torturous as what the Enemy had put Stone Claw's captive warriors through. Stone Claw's tattered men finally did appear at the valley's rim as the sun was peeking over the eastern edge of their world. The word of their return shot like lightning through the village. Everyone rushed out to meet them, and from various quarters came either cries of relief or the mournful wails for the lost loved ones. Mostly it was the later.

Their chief, at least, had returned, and that brought a measure of comfort and reassurance to the people. But the word he had brought back with him sent the people back into instant despair.

Mark Head was among those who went to meet the returning warriors. "What happened out there, Kit?"

"Stone Claw lost a lot of good men, but that ain't the half of it. Thar are more 'n thirty Diggers on our tail. I managed to stall them for a few hours, but they'll be here directly, and they ain't in any mood to smoke a pipe an' talk peace."

"Reckon it's time you and me pull out?"

"That's what a smart man might do," Kit agreed.

Mark frowned. "But that's not what you intend to do, is it, Kit?"

He grimaced. "I've sorta gotten attached to these folks, and now they're gonna need every gun we got. But I can't ask you to stay if you don't want to, Mark."

The frown lengthened and Mark said, "I know what you mean about these people. They're the friendliest Injuns I've met in a long while. What do you figure our odds?"

"How much powder you got left?"

Mark shook the polished buffalo horn that hung from his shoulder. "Maybe a dozen, maybe less."

"Whal, depending on how straight you an' me can shoot, and how long Stone Claw's few hale and hearty warriors can hold out against a passel of Diggers with scalp-taking in mind, I'd say we got even odds."

Mark grinned. "Fifty-fifty? Shoot, Kit, why didn't

your just say so. I don't start to worrying until the odds are tilted enough to capsize one of Fulton's newfangled steamboats. Fifty-fifty, that's just every-day-living odds most every place west of St. Louis."

"Kit!"

The trapper looked over as Night-Sky Feather ran past the others and threw her arms about his waist.

"I feared that you would not return. I asked Father Sun to bring you back safely."

"He brought me through by the skin of my teeth, and not much more," Kit answered, feeling somewhat conspicuous standing there in full sight of the village with Night-Sky Feather hugging him tightly. He caught a glimpse of Bone Breaker across the way. The warrior stared at them. Then, with his proud head dropping and his strong shoulders drooping a bit, he turned and stalked away toward the cliff lodges.

Kit quickly untangled himself from her arms and said, "Thar's lots we got to get done before warriors show up at your village."

"I know. Bone Breaker brought the chief's words to us earlier. We have filled every pot with water and brought stores of food into the lodges. The women are making arrows and the old warriors are fashioning spears."

Kit recalled Bone Breaker's forlorn look and asked, "Have you talked with Bone Breaker?"

She looked at him, surprised. "No. To speak to him for no reason would not be appropriate now that I am promised to you, Kit Carson," Night-Sky Feather explained as if that ought to have been obvious to him.

In spite of being flattered by her attentions and the glint of pride he saw in her eyes whenever she was with him, Kit couldn't help but feel a pang of regret for Bone Breaker. Bone Breaker's loss was his gain, and a lovely prize Night-Sky Feather was, but for some reason there was a deep, disquieting uneasiness within him—but its source was not a thing he could easily put a finger on . . . and at present not something that he had time to fully explore.

Kit told Night-Sky Feather to return to the other women and continue preparing the arrows while he and Mark went to confer with Stone Claw and the elders, who had gathered on the plaza of the cliff village, and were even now in earnest discussion.

"We should be leaving now, while we are still able to," Ghost Talker was saying. "The spirits of the ancestors have shown us the way we must go. It is foolish to remain here and fight when we still have time to flee."

"Where better to fight the Enemy than on our own ground?" Stone Claw countered. "Here at least we have protection behind these strong walls for our women, children, and old men. To flee now would only open us to attack while on the trail where there would be no place for the People to hide."

"Perhaps the Enemy would not follow if they arrive and find that we have already left."

Some of the elders agreed with Ghost Talker, while others came alongside the chief.

One of the elders said angrily, "My son was killed in the battle that Stone Claw has just fought. I want to avenge his blood by spilling much blood of the Enemy. I say we stand and fight!"

Another father spoke up with equal passion. "I too lost a brave son. But I do not want to stay here and watch his wife and his sons, my grandsons, die as well. I agree with Ghost Talker. The Enemy might not follow if they find the village already deserted."

Mark, who had been following the debate with some difficulty, said quietly at Kit's side, "If I know my Diggers like I think I do, they'll hound these people's trail until they've butchered every one of 'em."

"That's about the way I see it too, Mark."

A third man interrupted them. "Did not Bone Breaker say that their numbers are growing? That the Enemy has many tribes and that more warriors have joined with them?"

"It is true," Stone Claw admitted. "While I was a prisoner in their camp many men came from the place where Father Sun goes to his sleeping lodge. There is little hope that we can win a fight when their numbers increase while so many of our warriors have already passed over to Seguro's sleep world. But even so, to flee now and let them catch us in the open would mean certain death. At least here we have a small hope of success, for our lodges are strong and easily defended."

Reluctantly, the men agreed to the logic of that, although some still insisted that the Enemy would not follow them. Kit kept his thoughts to himself as it was not his place to interfere in these tribal matters. But when the decision to stay and fight was finally made, he gave a small sigh of relief. As Stone Claw had pointed out, their lodges were strong and easy to defend. There was no easy way down off the rim of the canyon into this valley, and so long as his and Mark's powder held out, shooting Diggers off the stark stone walls of this narrow valley would be easy as shooting ducks on a still pond.

But once their powder ran out . . .

Well, as Mark had said, fifty-fifty was everyday-living odds in this wild country. Kit just hoped he hadn't overestimated them too much this time.

"You're dragging your feet. Come on, time to head on back."

The half-breed Ute grimaced as he rolled up his blanket and oilcloth groundsheet. "I suppose I am, Gabe. I'm loath to give up the search." Gray Feather shrugged his shoulders as if finally admitting defeat to himself. "But it looks as if we've exhausted every possibility."

Jim Bridger lifted his saddle onto the horse's back, giving a small wince from the stab of pain in his own back. "I'm against leaving men behind, Gray Feather . . . maybe even more so than most. If I thought there was any chance of finding Kit and Mark alive I'd keep it up all summer. You've seen that river. It's wilder than a white b'ar with cubs. Gener'l Ashley led a party of trappers down it in bull boats back in '25, and they wrecked themselves on those rapids. How do you think Kit and Mark could have fared any better on a makeshift raft that would have broken upon going over the first cataract?"

"Men have survived worse fixes," the Indian observed, tying the bedroll behind his saddle. But now he was only thinking out loud, no longer trying to convince anyone, including himself.

Bridger grimaced. "Yep, I know all about that too," he said, his voice suddenly low and thoughtful.

All at once Gray Feather regretted having spoken of such things. His idle observation, he knew, had made Bridger recall that dark period in his life back in 1823 when as a nineteen-year-old kid he and another trapper named Fitzgerald had left the bear-mauled Hugh Glass alone and without his weapons to die in the wilderness.

"Let's get moving, Gabe. No use hanging around here any longer."

The men swung onto their mounts. Jim Bridger took the lead with Gray Feather's stout Indian pony falling in behind him. As they moved away from the canyon's rim, abandoning the search for their lost partners, a fist tightened within the Indian's breast. In the brief year that he had known Kit Carson they had become close friends, and leaving the search now was the same as admitting that the trapper was dead . . . one of the hardest things Gray Feather had ever had to do.

While the village was hastily preparing itself for the attack that could come at any time, Kit acquired a piece of rawhide from Night-Sky Feather with which to repair the crack in his rifle's stock. After soaking the leather in water and stretching and stitching it around the rifle's wrist, he set the gun in the sun to let the patch dry and shrink in place. Such expedient repairs were common in the wilderness where gunsmiths were few and far between, and generally, if done with care, would put the firearm back into as good a condition as before the break.

"Where the hell are they?" Mark asked, squinting against the bright sky at the canyon's rim.

"I'm not in any great hurry for 'em to come," Kit noted.

"It's the waiting that gets to me, Kit. I'd as soon go out and find 'em as to sit and wait for 'em."

"They'll be along," Kit said, eyeing the men below who, like Mark and himself, were now just waiting. There were fourteen altogether, with another dozen or so old men inside the lodges, armed with spears. Kit grinned to himself. It would be a prickly time for any Digger who wanted to get through the narrow doors to the women and children.

Mark grabbed his rifle. "Well, I best be getting over to the other side." He gave Kit a narrow glance. Then the twitch of a grin came to his ruddy face. "You shoot straight, Kit, and good luck to us all."

"You too, Mark," Kit replied as the trapper started down the ladder. They had decided that up high on either side of the canyon was the best place for two riflemen. Kit would remain on the terrace of the stone cliff lodges, while Mark was to station himself on a rocky ledge directly across the canyon. That way their cross fire would keep the steep rock walls picked clean of Diggers attempting to scramble down into the canyon . . . at least so long as powder and ball held out.

The morning was still early, yet any moment Kit expected to hear a war cry ring out from the canyon's rim. But minutes passed with nothing happening. In the valley below the cliff lodges, Stone Claw was circulating among his men, handing out strips of doeskin for each to tie about his forehead, and at the same time encouraging them. Encouragement was something everyone could use more of.

The hairs at the nape of Kit's neck tingled in anticipation. As more time passed his nerves grew taut, set like a hair trigger. . . .

A sound of footsteps on the terrace walkway behind him brought him instantly about, his rifle ready.

Ghost Talker stopped abruptly, startled at the sudden sight of the rifle's huge bore.

Kit grinned and raised the muzzle. "Sorry 'bout that, Ghost Talker."

The old man came forward, his deeply creased face expressionless, like a shriveled-up prune. But there was a spark of passion in those dark, intense eyes of his. "I must know," he said cryptically.

"Know?"

"The vision which the spirits showed to us. You seem to know of this place, the place where the ancestors went long ago. Is it true?"

Kit hadn't yet decided if what he had seen while down at the river had been real, or merely an illusion caused by the intoxicating tobacco that Ghost Talker had made him smoke. Yet there was no doubt that the old shaman had believed the visions. "I know the place that I saw, but if it is truly the place where your ancestors all went, I can't say for a certain. The more I think it over, the more the pieces all fit together. Including the language you speak."

"Where is this place, Kit Carson?"

"South of here is a river called the Rio Del Norte. Thar's a pueblo—a building sorta like your stone lodges only made of adobe brick—nearby the river where folks who speak your language now live. It's called Taos."

"Taos," the old man said as if locking the name safely away inside his head. Then he nodded gravely. "Then Taos is the place where we must go."

"The village is south and east of here a few hunder miles, over some of the mightiest mountains that the Good Lord ever did raise up. It's a long trek for old men and little children, but if you've a mind to go, then this is the time of year to do it."

"It is a time that has come," the shaman said firmly but soberly.

Kit didn't think he ought to mention that maybe the time had already passed them by. Unless the Diggers could be stopped here and now, and Stone Claw's people given the opportunity they needed to escape, there'd be no exodus to Taos, or anywhere else . . . except, perhaps, to this place the People called Seguro's sleep world.

Ghost Talker turned back and retraced his steps to one of the lodges where many of the women and children were kept, guarded by the older warriors who had been heavily armed with spears.

Below, Kit watched some of women—Night-Sky Feather among them—carrying bundles of sharpened sticks out to the warriors. When the fighting began, he hoped that they'd have the sense to retreat to the safety of the lodges. But knowing Indians as he did, he understood that women often fought alongside their men as valiantly as any of the warriors.

Kit grimaced at the thought that she could be killed along with the others, but before he could explore that unpleasant realization, a sudden whirring reached his ears. Kit knew the meaning of that sound at once. Instinctively he ducked his head. On the valley floor below one of the young warriors leaped up, staggered back, and fell dead with an arrow through his heart.

The next instant the canyon's rim rang with the blood-chilling war whoops from an army of throats. Everywhere Kit looked, half-naked men suddenly appeared, and with them a deadly rain of arrows fell upon Stone Claw's warriors down in the canyon.

Chapter Fifteen

Volley after volley of incoming arrows peppered the valley floor as Stone Claw's fighting men dove for cover from the deadly rain. Protected behind the rock walls of the cliff village, Kit settled his front sight on one of the distant warriors and pulled the trigger. As the Indian reeled headfirst into the deep canyon, the Diggers clambered back from the canyon's rim while still keeping up their steady barrage.

The boom of a rifle from across the valley told Kit that Mark had joined the fight.

This day the Enemy did not immediately start down into the canyon as they had on their previous attack, but remained on top just out of reach of the cliff villager's weapons. That last attack had taught them a hard lesson and they were not going to hastily repeat the error, Kit realized as he steadied his sights on another warrior. His rifle barked again, and high on the rim a second attacker disappeared.

These warriors might have been out of range of Stone Claw's arrows, but they were not beyond the long reach of the trappers' heavy buffalo guns. Just the same, it was not as simple as shooting ducks on a still lake, as Kit had hoped it might be. Each shot was long and uncertain, and with their gunpowder running low, Kit and Mark could not afford very many misses.

By now Stone Claw's warriors had all scrambled to cover, making the Diggers' downpour of arrows a useless exercise, and a waste of ammunition. All at once the deadly peppering ceased. Kit swiftly rammed another ball down the barrel of his rifle, waiting and knowing that the warriors up on the canyon's rim were about to change tactics. They had only one choice now. . . .

Kit scanned the many crevices that cut deep into the steep cliff walls. He was certain that the Diggers' next move would be to swarm into the canyon. As his gaze leaped along the rugged rock face, a movement in one of the declivities arrested his eyes.

They were starting down!

No clear shot immediately presented itself, so Kit hunkered down and waited, squinting along the barrel of his rifle until a dusky figure flashed into view. Kit touched the trigger and across the valley a puff of gray dust arose where the bullet had slammed into rock outcropping. Cursing beneath his breath, Kit quickly reloaded and settled down again to wait.

Mark's rifle boomed from the other side of the canyon, but the results were uncertain. Below, Stone Claw's men were scurrying into position. They too knew what was about to happen.

All at once a pair of bold Diggers tried to beat the rifle fire over the rim of the canyon to the west. Kit drew a bead and plucked one from the rock wall. Mark picked off the other, but as the two trappers raced to reload their rifles, a dozen more warriors took advantage and scurried down the rock face, using the hand and toe holes carved there generations ago. Now the Diggers were pouring into the valley from all directions, and Kit's rifle barrel grew hot as a flapjack griddle as he fired and reloaded, and fired again.

Stone Claw's men engaged the enemy on the valley floor where they were outnumbered three to one—even with Kit and Mark evening up the odds some. After a few minutes no more Diggers appeared on the canyon's rim; they were all in the canyon. As the warriors clashed below, the trappers had to take particular care not to hit the men from the cliff village. At Kit's suggestion, Stone Claw had issued each of his warriors a headband of pale doeskin so that Kit and Mark could distinguish the cliff warriors from the Enemy; a tactic that Colonel Henry Leavenworth had employed some twelve years earlier upon enlisting the help of several hundred Sioux warriors in a botched attempt to punish a strong, stockaded Arikara village on the Missouri River.

Then Kit's powder ran out.

He left his rifle on the terrace, clambered down the spindly ladders, and dashed out onto the valley floor to engage the enemy hand to hand. The first Indian to come his way buckled from a blow of Kit's tomahawk. As the man crumpled, Kit snatched away his war lance and, wheeling about, drove its long iron point through the naked chest of a second Digger. The battle raged on around all him and in

149

the heat of it, time seemed to stand still. Kit was only distantly aware that Mark's rifle had fallen silent too, but whether his powder had run out or a Digger warrior had gotten to him, Kit had no way of knowing.

Some of the village women were rushing across the battlefield with bundles of sharpened sticks to resupply the men. One woman was cut down by a Digger's war lance, and another fell with an arrow through her chest.

At the whistle of an arrow coming in, Kit threw himself to the ground, rolled, and sprang back to his feet, coming face-to-face with two more warriors. One of the Diggers lunged with his iron-tipped war lance. Kit's tomahawk flashed out and cut the weapon in half. At the same time, crouching low, he drove his big butcher knife into the man's gut. Wrenching it free, Kit came about and threw up a block as the second warrior's heavy club came down and clanked against the hickory shaft of Kit's tomahawk. Kit turned from under it, and his short ax struck out and opened a gash between the man's lower ribs, cutting deep into his right side.

A glimpse of buckskin and fringe flying through the intervening scrubby growth told Kit that Mark had joined the battle. How long they could hold out against these greater odds was a question whose answer held anything but the promise of a long and bright future for either of the mountain men—or those warriors of Stone Claw who still remained standing.

Stone Claw! At that moment Kit saw the chief fending off three men.

Stone Claw was staggering back, his defenses crumbling under the weight of the pressing Diggers. His face and chest were red with blood, some of it his own and some the badges of victory over many of the Enemy. But the chief was not a young man and the battle was rapidly wearing him down. All around him the beleaguered cliff warriors battled two, sometimes three opponents at once, and one by one fell beneath the overwhelming odds.

Kit started towards Stone Claw, cutting a path of blood that left three more Diggers writhing upon the dusty canyon floor. Just then Night-Sky Feather dashed into view, fleet of foot, a stone-tipped war lance clutched in her fist, and raven hair streaming loose behind her as she flew across the rocky ground. She managed to expertly dodge the first couple of Diggers who rose up before her as she obstinately made her way to the faltering chief.

Kit shifted direction and put himself on course to intercept her. To his left a Digger was drawing back his bow. Without breaking stride, Kit flung his butcher knife. The man gasped and released the arrow, sending it harmlessly over Night-Sky Feather's head.

Suddenly a pair of snarling warriors leaped in her path and confronted her. She wheeled to a stop, clutching the lance in both hands, trying to keep the two cagey men in front of her covered. Moving swiftly, one of the warriors snatched the shaft of the spear and wrenched it away from Night-Sky Feather while the other sprang for her neck. At that same moment Kit leaped to the top of a boulder and launched himself for the nearest man. A hideous war cry escaped the trapper's throat as his tomahawk struck.

The warrior's skull cracked beneath the ax and as his legs crumpled in death, Kit turned his attention to the second fellow, who wielded a tomahawk of his own. The two men circled each other once, but before either one could make his move, the Digger suddenly gasped, let out a muffled cry, and fell face forward, dead at Kit's feet.

Night-Sky Feather gave a tug and yanked the spear point from the man's back.

"Get back with the other women!" Kit ordered.

"My father needs help," she answered determinedly, her breath coming in short gasps.

Somehow, he didn't think she'd be easy to convince, and this was not the time or place to try.

"Look!" she cried, pointing.

Stone Claw had gone down beneath the weapons of the Enemy and one of the Diggers was raising his war club for the killing blow. But before he could administer it Bone Breaker was suddenly in their midst, swinging his stone-tipped club with the fury of a she-bear defending her young. Stone Claw managed to scoot back from under the Diggers and, grabbing up his spear, he drove it clear through one of the warriors.

Seeing that Stone Claw was down, more Diggers rallied to the side of their comrades. The battle was just about over, and all that remained to make it complete was to kill the chief. Though their numbers had been hacked back to a less than a quarter of what they had begun with, victory was easily within the Enemy's grasp, and there was little the few remaining defenders could do to prevent it.

"Go back to the lodges now!" Kit ordered Night-Sky Feather, and the tone in his voice left no room for a discussion on the matter. Six long strides placed Kit at Bone Breaker's elbow, and together they threw up a wall between the Enemy and Stone Claw, who was still struggling to climb back to his feet. The chief bore a dozen wounds and was weakening swiftly from the rigors of the battle and the loss of blood.

Fighting wildly, nearly blinded by the flow of sweat into his eyes, Kit struck and dodged and parried as if by sheer instinct. Then a woman's cry of alarm rang out. With a quick glance past the warriors who had mounted against him, Kit saw that two Diggers had grabbed Night-Sky Feather and were hauling the struggling girl away from the village toward the cliffs where another man was signaling to them. The mountain man tried to break free of his attackers, but they forced him back.

Bone Breaker had heard her cry too and with a Herculean effort, and wild rage burning in his dark eyes, he burst through the battle lines and plunged recklessly past the few remaining skirmishes, his heavy stone battle club wheeling like the vanes of a windmill before a furious wind.

Their unyielding onslaught had pressed Kit and Stone Claw ever backward until the canyon wall loomed up behind them. Then Kit's heel caught the gnarled root of a stunted juniper, but an instant before he tripped he had a glimpse of Bone Breaker's clash with the Diggers who were trying to carry off Night-Sky Feather. In that instant the brave cliff warrior was truly living up to his name. Then the mountain man fell beneath the crush of the Enemy, and with his muscles aching, his strength ebbing, and their murderous weapons closing in on him, he knew that he had finally come to his end—he and these friendly cliff folks as well. . . .

Just as on that morning only a handful of days past, when he had clawed his way half drowned out of the river onto the stony bank and had passed out,

Kit once again had that eerie feeling that he was in the presence of a deity. Only now, instead of peering into his blinding countenance, Kit was hearing his booming voice. . . .

And just as on that morning, exhaustion and the nearness of death had played a trick with his senses. If it was the voice of a deity booming down through the canyon, the words sure packed a wallop!

The first Digger was knocked aside as if by a powerful fist, and as a second startled warrior looked up, the invisible fist struck out again and punched him to the ground. The fist, and the booming of a buffalo rifle coming at about the same time, straightened out the confusion in Kit's brain quicker than bear grease off a hot rock.

The sharp reports from a brace of pistols echoed down from the canyon's rim, and an instant later a pair of Diggers stumbled. One managed to regain his footing and dashed for cover, but the other remained stretched out on the ground stone-still, except for the pool of blood spreading thickly across his chest.

With renewed vigor, Kit charged the scattering warriors. Another boom of a rifle sent a fleeing Digger on his way to the ghosts of his ancestors. Kit spied the puff of white high above, and the smudge of buckskin as the man up there quickly reloaded. Not far away a second rifle belched smoke, and somewhere below another Digger crossed over the river.

The near-victory turned instantly into a full-scale rout with Diggers fleeing for cover wherever it could be found. There was no way of knowing how many mountain men had arrived, but from the sound of rifles and pistols, to the Diggers at least, it must have seemed like a fearful lot! In spite of all the gunfire, however, Kit had already determined it was coming from just two locations.

It then occurred to Kit that some of the cliff warriors were in danger of being shot. Striding out in the open, he called for the cliff warriors to gather around him. Stone Claw staggered alongside Kit, and from various quarters those men who were still on their feet and able to walk came to their chief's side. Bone Breaker guided a bewildered Night-Sky Feather along with him as the last of the Diggers fled down the valley toward the river.

Chapter Sixteen

On the rim of the canyon one of the two trappers stood and waved an arm. It was Jim Bridger! And the other man, Kit was pleased to discover, was Gray Feather!

From out of a thicket emerged a battle-weary but grinning Mark Head, limping slightly as he stumbled across to the gathering place, a bloodied tomahawk clutched in his fist.

"Who are they?" he asked, shading his eyes and squinting at the place where the men had appeared. By now the two trappers had moved out of sight, on their way down into the canyon.

"It's Bridger and Gray Feather," Kit answered.

"You don't say! Well, I reckon that Injun *can* shoot after all."

"I told you so, didn't I?" Kit was suddenly in high spirits. They had beaten back the Diggers—with a little help—and chances were good the Enemy would not be back any time soon. Then his view found Bone Breaker with Night-Sky Feather standing at his side. A frown tightened Kit's face and pushed the grin aside. "I reckon thar's still something I got to take care of," he said, sobering up.

As he approached Bone Breaker, Night-Sky Feather stepped away from the warrior's side to the short but proper distance required of a woman promised to another man. Yet Kit sensed that a change had come over her. If she had ever questioned Bone Breaker's affections in the past, there could be no doubting them now. To have seen the zeal with which he had come to her rescue was to have seen the ardor that burned in his heart for this young woman. She would have to have been blind not to have noticed.

It was plain, also, that Night-Sky Feather's infatuation with Kit was fading—even as her apprehension was growing. And Kit figured he knew what was running wild through her brain now. What would become of her in this strange white man's world where men command thunder and wore clothes made of colorful skins that had come from no animal she had ever seen? To taste forbidden fruits always held its allure. But to make a regular meal of them, well, that was something else altogether. Something that maybe Night-Sky Feather was discovering she wasn't really ready for yet.

But for many cultures, traditions are unbreakable chains that bind forever. Night-Sky Feather was bound by the traditions of hers.

Kit said, "A lot of your people died, Bone Breaker, and I'm right sorry 'bout that, but we sent them Diggers on the run now."

Bone Breaker's face remained unmoving as he nodded toward the canyon's rim where Bridger and

Gray Feather had showed up. "Those men with the thunder sticks, they are clansmen of yours?"

"You might say that. We're partners. Mr. Jim Bridger and Mr. Waldo Gray Feather Smith is thar names. They must have been looking for Mark and me after we was swept away down that wild river. You can say one thing for them. They picked a good time to find us."

"Now that they have come, you will go away with them?" Night-Sky Feather asked.

"Reckon I will." Kit glanced up toward the cliff lodges as the women, children, and old men began to emerge. "I suspect you folks will be leaving too, if Ghost Talker has his way about it. He seems to think it's time for you all to go and join up with them who went before you, and I ain't sure he ain't right about that."

Stone Claw walked stiffly over, a hand clamped tightly over a bleeding wound in his side. "It is true, we will follow the words of Ghost Talker. He has learned where the ancestors who left long ago have gone. We have no other choice now, for if we stay here the Enemy will return with many more of his warriors. We are too few now, and can fight no more."

"Whal, I think it's the right move for you. Them Diggers are only off licking thar wounds. They'll be back before long with all thar kinsmen, and madder than King George after that night when a company of patriots went and dumped a boatload of his tea in Boston Harbor."

Stone Claw turned to Bone Breaker. "Tell the people to make preparations to leave. We must be on our way many days before the Enemy returns."

The young warrior hesitated and glanced at Night-Sky Feather. There was sudden urgency and passion in his eyes. Then, with a small wince of resignation that pulled heavily at his face, he lowered his head to his chest and started off to do the chief's bidding.

"Hold up thar a minute, Bone Breaker," Kit said.

The warrior looked back. In spite of their differences at first, Kit had come to respect this man's loyalty, and his bravery. And then there was Night-Sky Feather. She was a daughter of the past. To take her away from her people would be sort of like plucking a flower out of the dawn of time and trying to fit it into a world becoming so confounded mechanical that it even baffled Kit Carson at times to think of it. How could he ever explain to a person who had known only stone knives and bearskins the notion of forged steal, steam power, and fine cotton cloth produced in English mills across a vast ocean, thousands of miles away from Louisiana where the cotton had been grown. Oh, it could be done. It had been done. But did he want to do it? For Night-Sky Feather, these things would be best learned in the familiar company of her own people.

Kit said, "You're a mighty brave warrior, Bone Breaker. One of the finest I've ever known. I'd welcome you to fight at my side anytime. But I reckon this here is good-bye. Between Stone Claw and you, I have no doubts your people will make it to wherever it is you're going, and if you end up in Taos, whal, then I'll look you up the next time I'm thar and see how you done."

He looked at Night-Sky Feather. "You're about the prettiest gal I've laid eyes on since leaving civilization, and any man would be right proud to call you his wife. But the sad fact is, I'm not much for settling down—at least not yet. Thar's a big old canyon down south of here that I've a hankering to see, and I'm bound to be going back to Californee a time or two, and when I do maybe I'll wander on up north and have me a good long look at that thar Columbia River what I've heard so much about.

"On the other hand, thar are folks here who would miss you fiercely if you went away." Kit glanced at Bone Breaker, then back. "Reckon what I'm trying to say is that whatever obligation you figure you owe because I saved your life, whal, I'm not goin' to hold you to it. You belong here with your people, and with Bone Breaker. He's gonna need you more than ever now that you all are leaving this place."

Bone Breaker's eyes momentarily brightened; then the glimmer faded. Night-Sky Feather's face seemed even unhappier than it had a moment before. Kit wondered what error he had committed now. But it was Stone Claw who broke the uneasy silence.

"This cannot be," he said flatly. "My daughter belongs to the man who kept her from Seguro's sleep world. It is way of the People."

Kit frowned. *Confound thar traditions!* Then a thought occurred to him and suddenly he grinned. "Whal, then that settles it, I reckon. Night-Sky Feather don't even belong to me anymore. Why, if it warn't for ol' Bone Breaker thar, them Diggers would've killed Night-Sky Feather practically where she stood. I seen it with my own eyes. They grabbed her up and thar was murder in thar faces if I ever seen such before—and believe me, I've seen a passel of murderous looks in my day. Bone Breaker leaped to her rescue and fought them warriors like he was a wild painter! If anyone ever snatched your daughter from the grasp of this Seguro fellow, why, it was Bone Breaker thar."

Stone Claw looked at the young warrior. "This is true?"

Bone Breaker was bright enough to recognize that Kit had opened a door for them, and immediately he stepped through it. "Yes, what the pale stranger says is true."

Stone Claw was momentarily at a loss. Kit figured the rules had been set up for a rescue happening only once; twice in a row was something that the chief had obviously not run into before. "I must consult Ghost Talker," Stone Claw hedged finally.

"Whal, I can't wait around much longer and neither can you. You're chief of these people, you can make the decision right here and now," Kit prodded.

Stone Claw thought it over, then nodded his head. "Yes, it must be so."

Kit knew that deep down in his heart, it was the decision that Stone Claw had wanted to make all along.

Both Bone Breaker and Night-Sky Feather came out of their melancholy, and as if each had become suddenly magnetized, they moved together.

"Now go tell the others to pack everything. We must be on our way soon," Stone Claw said.

As the two cliff people hurried toward the village, Kit looked back at Stone Claw. "It was the right thing."

"Was it? When we abandon our home, do we also leave our beliefs behind?" The chief went off to help the wounded, although he was hurt as badly as any of the warriors there, leaving Kit with that thought to ponder.

Bridger and Gray Feather strode up with Mark coming alongside them. "Figured you two for dead men," Bridger said stone faced. "If it wasn't for

Gray Feather I'd have given up the search days ago."

"How'd you ever find us, Gabe, tucked down in this here canyon like we are?"

"We were on our way out to meet up with the others when Gray Feather heard your gunfire a way off in the distance. He's got ears like a hoot owl's got eyes."

Mark leaned on the barrel of his rifle. "Reckon you was right about the Injun, Kit. He turned out to be all right."

"Told you he was handy to have around."

"Here I go, feeling like a pronoun again," Gray Feather complained.

For just a moment Bridger allowed a grin to touch his lips before quickly pulling them back into a tight, grim line. He looked around at the villagers gathering up their wounded, and the women coming from the cliff lodges to tend to their injuries.

"Who are these people? Don't reckon as I've ever seen anything much like this place," he said, his sharp eyes scanning the stone dwellings tucked back into the high cliffs.

Kit grimaced. "I haven't got it all figured out yet, Gabe, but near as I can reckon it, this here is a tribe that somehow got overlooked by Father Time when he was winnowing this here countryside. They talked a lot about thar ancestors having gone off somewhere long ago. I got the feeling these folks were left behind for some reason, but now they've gonna have to move on."

"A lost tribe, and a lost people," Gray Feather said whimsically, as if the notion had stirred something deep inside him.

"Reckon that's what they are. Lost folks just trying to find thar way home now."

*   *   *

Early the next morning the People gathered on the canyon's floor among the fields of tilled earth. Some of the garden patches were still only bare, fertile soil; others wore a tinge of bright green where young plants were beginning to come up— crops that would never be harvested. The People— those who had not been wounded in the battle —had loaded all their possessions onto their backs, a pitifully small collection of pots, baskets, skins, food, and farming tools. A meager showing, Kit thought sadly, considering that this had been their home for hundreds, maybe thousands of years.

The injured warriors among them would make their exodus from the valley slow going. To give Stone Claw's people a solid start on their long trek south, the trappers had promised to linger an extra day among the deserted cliff lodges against the possibility that the Diggers might return. But no one really expected the Enemy to mount another attack so soon.

Ghost Talker came through the small crowd, his skull-crowned walking staff stabbing the ground with each step, a leather sack slung over his shoulder. "Kit Carson," he said, setting the sack upon a stone and opening it. "I have a gift I wish to give to you." He rummaged through the sack.

"Shucks, Ghost Talker, you don't have to give me a present. I didn't do anything special."

"Ah, but you did. You touched the spirit world of my people. It was through you that we now know where the ancestors went." He withdrew a small skin pouch and presented it to Kit. "Here, this is for you."

"Whal, thank you. What is it?"

"The spirit smoke. Perhaps through it you too

163

might talk to the ancestors of your people."

Kit ruefully recalled the distorted visions down at the river, the weird colors, the grotesque shapes, the stomach-turning recovery some hours later when he'd finally come out of the smoke's stranglehold. But not wanting to offend the old man, Kit graciously accepted the gift.

Ghost Talker grinned and removed a small jar from the bag. From the sound it made, Kit suspected the vessel contained a small amount of water. "The spirits of our ancestors will come with us," he said happily, holding up the pot. "There is no need for them to remain here any longer."

"That's right thoughtful of you," was all Kit could manage, momentarily at a loss for words as he stared at the small vessel. "Ain't it gonna get cramped in thar for all them ghosts?"

But the old shaman appeared not to catch the skepticism in Kit's voice, and merely looked satisfied with himself as he carefully returned the pot to the bag and packed soft rabbit fur around it. As Ghost Talker made his way back to the villagers who were about to depart, Stone Claw stopped by to say his farewell.

"We will go now. Maybe someday our lives will cross again."

"I'll look you up the next time I get back to Taos."

Stone Claw nodded. "We will go there and if Father Sun and Father Moon smile on us, the grandchildren of our ancestors will remember us and take us into their lodges."

"Good luck. Keep an eye on your back trail, Stone Claw, and when the river forks to the east, that's the way you should go. East and south is where your destination lays."

Stone Claw handed Kit a feather that he had been holding. "My daughter asked me to give this to you. She says to think of her whenever you look at it."

Taking it, Kit glanced into the crowd. Night-Sky Feather was standing beside Bone Breaker, and Kit knew that was as it should be. At his glance, she decorously averted her eyes—and that was as it should be also. Some traditions were mighty hard chains to break. And after having thought over Stone Claw's words of the previous day, Kit had decided that some were even important enough to hold onto when the rest of your world seemed to be falling down around your ears.

"Thank you, Stone Claw. Tell Night-Sky Feather that I will not forget her, and tell her that I wish her all the best. I know she has picked a good man. May Night-Sky Feather and Bone Breaker give you many strong grandchildren."

The chief grinned and nodded his head in agreement.

Within the hour the whole village had climbed to the high ridge and had started their long trek south. Without them, the canyon seemed suddenly old and withered, as if their leaving had drained all the life from it. Even the stone lodges seemed suddenly to have grown old and dusty.

"What you got there?" Bridger asked when Kit had rejoined them near the spindly ladders that ran up to the now empty lodges.

Kit looked at the pouch of tobacco and the feather. "Gifts from the shaman and Night-Sky Feather."

"You're gonna miss that gal, I can see it already," Mark said, grinning. "You should have kept her when you had the chance."

But Kit knew he had done the right thing. Hefting the pouch, he suddenly squelched a smirk and handed it to Jim Bridger. "Here you go, Gabe. Pack your pipe with some of that. I guarantee it'll wipe that sour pucker from your face in less than five minutes."

Bridger's eyes hitched over at Kit suspiciously as he took the gift a little uncertainly. "Thanks, I'm running a little low of tobacco."

"It starts off with some kind of bite, Gabe, but just puff on through it. After a while you won't even notice. It'll be a smoke you'll never forget, and that's a fact."

"Think I'll have some now," Bridger said, fishing out his pipe. "Anyone care to join me?"

"No!" Mark said at once, obviously recalling his sampling of the stuff down in the ceremonial chamber. Then, softening his reply a little, he added, "Now that we've got powder again, I was just about to go see if I can't shoot us some dinner." He grabbed up his rifle and, giving Kit a wink, started off down the canyon.

"How 'bout you, Gray Feather?"

"Not now. Maybe later."

Kit said to the Ute, "Thar's something I want to show you down by the river."

"What's that?"

"The water down thar has a peculiar way about it. I figured you being a man with college schoolin' and all, you might know what's causing it."

"I'll come take a look."

The two men followed the long, narrow trail down to the bank of the Green River where Ghost Talker had summoned the spirits of the ancestors. But when Kit stepped out onto the ledge of rock overlooking the water, he couldn't see that odd luminosity anywhere.

"Whal, now that's a queer thing."

"What is, Kit?"

"You can't see it anymore, Gray Feather, but the other day this whole stretch of river appeared strange, sort of spring-green and bubbly, like thar was a hundred campfires burning beneath the water."

"That's impossible," Gray Feather said, stepping up alongside Kit and staring at the swift water.

"I know that! Why do you think I brought you down here, dadgumit!" Kit stared hard at the water again, but whatever had been there before was not there now.

"Maybe it was the light?" Gray Feather suggested. "You know how light has a way of playing tricks on a man. Especially far down in a canyon like this."

"Maybe," Kit answered, turning away from the river. But deep down inside he knew there had to be more to it than that. As they started back up the trail toward the cliff village he recalled what Night-Sky Feather had told him about Seguro snatching folks from the rocks and dragging them down into his dreaded "sleep world."

Only stories parents tell their kids to keep them away from the dangerously fast water, he recalled telling Night-Sky Feather.

Then Kit remembered the old shaman proudly showing him the pot of water and telling him that he was taking the ghosts of their ancestors with them on their journey south.

Could it be . . . ?

Kit glanced back at the river, which looked exactly like a river ought to look. He shook his head. No, it was only the old superstitions of a people who had outlived their time, he told himself firmly as he and Gray Feather made their way back to the canyon of empty cliff lodges.

Or was it?

KIT CARSON

DOUG HAWKINS

The frontier adventures of a true American legend.

#1: *The Colonel's Daughter.* Christopher "Kit" Carson is a true American legend: He can shoot a man at twenty paces, trap and hunt better than the most skilled Indians, and follow any trail—even in the dead of night. His courage and strength as an Indian fighter have earned him respect throughout the West. But all of his skills are put to the test when he gets caught up in a manhunt no one wants him to make. The beautiful daughter of a Missouri colonel has been taken by a group of trappers heading for the mountains, and Kit is determined to find her—even if he has to risk his life to do it!

___4295-9 $3.99 US/$4.99 CAN

Dorchester Publishing Co., Inc.
P.O. Box 6640
Wayne, PA 19087-8640

Please add $1.75 for shipping and handling for the first book and $.50 for each book thereafter. NY, NYC, and PA residents, please add appropriate sales tax. No cash, stamps, or C.O.D.s. All orders shipped within 6 weeks via postal service book rate. Canadian orders require $2.00 extra postage and must be paid in U.S. dollars through a U.S. banking facility.

Name_____
Address_____
City_____ State_____ Zip_____
I have enclosed $_____ in payment for the checked book(s).
Payment <u>must</u> accompany all orders. ☐ Please send a free catalog.

DON'T MISS THESE OTHER GREAT STORIES IN

THE LOST WILDERNESS TALES

DODGE TYLER

In the days of the musket, the powder horn, and the flintlock, one pioneer ventures forth into the virgin land that will become the United States.

#5: Apache Revenge. A band of Apaches with blood in their eyes ride the warpath right to Dan'l's door, looking to avenge their humiliating defeat at his hands three years earlier. And when they capture Dan'l's niece as a trophy it becomes more than just a battle for Dan'l, it becomes personal. No matter where the warriors ride, the frontiersman swears to find them, to get the girl back—and to exact some vengeance of his own.

_4183-9 $4.99 US/$5.99 CAN

#4: Winter Kill. Gold fever—the treacherous disease caused the vicious ends of many pioneers. One winter, Dan'l finds himself making a dangerous trek for lost riches buried in lands held sacred by the Sioux. Soon, Boone is fighting with all his skill and cunning to win a battle against hostile Sioux warriors, ferocious animals, and a blizzard that would bury a lesser man in a horrifying avalanche of death.

_4087-5 $4.99 US/$5.99 CAN

Dorchester Publishing Co., Inc.
P.O. Box 6640
Wayne, PA 19087-8640

Please add $1.75 for shipping and handling for the first book and $.50 for each book thereafter. NY, NYC, and PA residents, please add appropriate sales tax. No cash, stamps, or C.O.D.s. All orders shipped within 6 weeks via postal service book rate. Canadian orders require $2.00 extra postage and must be paid in U.S. dollars through a U.S. banking facility.

Name_____
Address_____
City_____ State_____ Zip_____
I have enclosed $_____ in payment for the checked book(s).
Payment <u>must</u> accompany all orders. ❑ Please send a free catalog.

DON'T MISS DAVID THOMPSON'S OTHER TITLES IN THE

Blood Rage. No pioneer knows the wilderness like the legendary Davy Crockett, but sometimes his curiosity leads him into more trouble than he expects. When Davy sees the tracks of a solitary wagon heading into the uncharted plains, he follows them to make sure the travelers know what they're in for. But the brave frontiersman doesn't know that the trail leads straight to savage Pawnee warriors out for blood.

___4316-5 $3.99 US/$4.99 CAN

Mississippi Mayhem. Davy's wanderlust keeps life interesting...but this time it may be a little too interesting. When the pioneer and his friend Flavius decide to canoe down the Mississippi, they don't count on running into hardcases out to grab everything they have, hostile Indians who want Davy's scalp, and an old Indian myth that turns out to be all too real.

___4278-9 $3.99 US/$4.99 CAN

Dorchester Publishing Co., Inc.
P.O. Box 6640
Wayne, PA 19087-8640

Please add $1.75 for shipping and handling for the first book and $.50 for each book thereafter. NY, NYC, and PA residents, please add appropriate sales tax. No cash, stamps, or C.O.D.s. All orders shipped within 6 weeks via postal service book rate. Canadian orders require $2.00 extra postage and must be paid in U.S. dollars through a U.S. banking facility.

Name_____
Address_____
City_____State_____Zip_____
I have enclosed $_____ in payment for the checked book(s).
Payment <u>must</u> accompany all orders. ☐ Please send a free catalog.

DOUBLE EDITION
Blood Bounty/The Trackers
Jake McMasters

Blood Bounty. The settlers believe Clay Taggart is a ruthless desperado. The army says he should be left to rot under the desert sun. But Taggart is an innocent man with a bounty on his hide. With a motley band of Apaches, he roams the vast Southwest, waiting for the day he can clear his name, fighting any bounty hunter foolish enough to take him on.

And in the same action-packed volume...

The Trackers. When a bloodthirsty trio comes after the White Apache and his followers, prepared to slaughter them like sheep, they don't know that Clay Taggart isn't about to let anyone kill him.

___4318-1 $4.99 US/$5.99 CAN

Dorchester Publishing Co., Inc.
P.O. Box 6640
Wayne, PA 19087-8640

Please add $1.75 for shipping and handling for the first book and $.50 for each book thereafter. NY, NYC, and PA residents, please add appropriate sales tax. No cash, stamps, or C.O.D.s. All orders shipped within 6 weeks via postal service book rate. Canadian orders require $2.00 extra postage and must be paid in U.S. dollars through a U.S. banking facility.

Name_____
Address_____
City_____ State_____ Zip_____
I have enclosed $_____ in payment for the checked book(s).
Payment <u>must</u> accompany all orders. ❏ Please send a free catalog.

CHEYENNE

DOUBLE EDITION
JUDD COLE

One man's heroic search for a world he can call his own.

Arrow Keeper. A Cheyenne raised among pioneers, Matthew Hanchon has never known anything but distrust. The settlers brand him a savage, and when Matthew realizes that his adopted parents will suffer for his sake, he flees into the wilderness—where he'll need a warrior's courage if he hopes to survive.

And in the same volume...

Death Chant. When Matthew returns to the Cheyenne, he doesn't find the acceptance he seeks. The Cheyenne can't fully trust any who were raised in the ways of the white man. Forced to prove his loyalty, Matthew faces the greatest challenge he has ever known.

___4280-0 $4.99 US/$5.99 CAN

Dorchester Publishing Co., Inc.
P.O. Box 6640
Wayne, PA 19087-8640

Please add $1.75 for shipping and handling for the first book and $.50 for each book thereafter. NY, NYC, and PA residents, please add appropriate sales tax. No cash, stamps, or C.O.D.s. All orders shipped within 6 weeks via postal service book rate. Canadian orders require $2.00 extra postage and must be paid in U.S. dollars through a U.S. banking facility.

Name_____
Address_____
City_____State_____Zip_____
I have enclosed $_____ in payment for the checked book(s).
Payment <u>must</u> accompany all orders. ❑ Please send a free catalog.

"Max Brand practices his art to something like perfection!"
—*The New York Times*

MAX BRAND

THE DESERT PILOT/ VALLEY OF JEWELS

TWO WESTERN CLASSICS IN PAPERBACK FOR THE FIRST TIME!

The Desert Pilot. The town of Billman is known for its lawlessness, but Reverend Reginald Ingram arrives with high hopes to defeat the power of the saloons and gunsmoke. But soon the preacher may have to choose between his peaceful ways and survival.

And in the same volume...

Valley of Jewels. Beautiful Daggett Valley is pitted with danger. Here Buck Logan plots to con a half-witted old man into revealing where he has hidden a cache of jewels, but schemes don't always go according to plan, and before the end of the day, blood will be shed.

___4315-7 $4.99 US/$5.99 CAN

Dorchester Publishing Co., Inc.
P.O. Box 6640
Wayne, PA 19087-8640

Please add $1.75 for shipping and handling for the first book and $.50 for each book thereafter. NY, NYC, and PA residents, please add appropriate sales tax. No cash, stamps, or C.O.D.s. All orders shipped within 6 weeks via postal service book rate. Canadian orders require $2.00 extra postage and must be paid in U.S. dollars through a U.S. banking facility.

Name_____
Address_____
City_____ State_____ Zip_____
I have enclosed $_____ in payment for the checked book(s).
Payment <u>must</u> accompany all orders. ☐ Please send a free catalog.

BONNER'S STALLION
T. V. OLSEN

Winner of the Golden Spur Award

Bonner's life is the kind that makes a man hard, makes him love the high country, and makes him fear nothing but being limited by another man's fenceposts. Suddenly it looks as if his life is going to get even harder. He has already lost his woman. Now he is about to lose his son and his mountain ranch to a rich and powerful enemy—a man who hates to see any living thing breathing free. That is when El Diablo Rojo, the feared and hated rogue stallion, comes back into Bonner's life. He and Bonner have one thing in common...they are survivors.

___4276-2 $4.50 US/$5.50 CAN

Dorchester Publishing Co., Inc.
P.O. Box 6640
Wayne, PA 19087-8640

Please add $1.75 for shipping and handling for the first book and $.50 for each book thereafter. NY, NYC, and PA residents, please add appropriate sales tax. No cash, stamps, or C.O.D.s. All orders shipped within 6 weeks via postal service book rate. Canadian orders require $2.00 extra postage and must be paid in U.S. dollars through a U.S. banking facility.

Name_____
Address_____
City_____State_____Zip_____
I have enclosed $_____ in payment for the checked book(s).
Payment <u>must</u> accompany all orders. ❏ Please send a free catalog.

ATTENTION WESTERN CUSTOMERS!

SPECIAL TOLL-FREE NUMBER
1-800-481-9191

Call Monday through Friday
12 noon to 10 p.m.
Eastern Time
*Get a free catalogue,
join the Western Book Club,
and order books using your
Visa, MasterCard,
or Discover®*

*Leisure
Books*